PRICE OF MEN

Book 1 - Temporary Forevers

LENWARD DOUGLAS

This is a work of fiction. Similarities to real people, places, or events are entirely coincidental.

Published by HUSTLAS HOPE PUBLISHING GROUP, INC.
Cover art by Nicki D Davis.
Music lyrics are licensed through HUSTLAS HOPE MUSIC INTERNATIONAL.

For more information regarding permission, send an email to Hustlashopepublishinggroup@gmail.com

Contents

ACKNOWLEDGMENT

Special thanks to my friends at Tri-State Corporation for all the support. My guys from the cutting department, much love and respect. Ms.Knuckles for allowing me the space to work. Yah Ya for holding it down in the mountains with me; forever love and respect.

My family, we are stronger together.

#Jlifematters Joshua Dashield, always in my heart, brother. Ms. Leila, always my love.

PROLOGUE

Frank McDaniel is a 25-year veteran of the Philadelphia Police Force. He spent his first eight years as a street cop, eleven years in homicide, and is now in his 6th year as head of the narcotics division. At 52 years old, Frank could have retired but being an alcoholic, a two-time divorce, a single father, and $75,000 in gambling debt. The police force was all he had. It was the life that flowed through his veins and pumped through his heart, aside from all the cigarette smoke and Irish whiskey. It was his balance of power.

Fresh off a 3 to 11 shift, Frank makes his first of two rounds. A visit to a speakeasy called Jiggas. Jiggas is notoriously known in the underground as Sin city. Located in Southwest Philadelphia on the 1700 block of Conestoga St. Its three connected row houses with the interior walls knocked down to combine them into one. A one-stop shop for everything exclusive and exotic, from drug trafficking to sex trafficking and everything in between, supported and funded by a secret clientele of the most elite and corrupt characters that the Tri-State had to offer.

Frank's business at Jiggas tonight was on behalf of the police commissioner, to collect $50,000, a service tax to keep the heat off Jiggas, and a courtesy call whenever the F.B.I or immigration picked something up off the grape vine.

Frank was a throwback, a cop from the era where when a hand went over fist, a blind eye was cast. He wasn't above taking money for aiding an illegal business to operate. Doing so, he built a reputation and mutual respect for the underworld and his former partner and newly elected police commissioner David Cameron.

Fuck the moral code of the law. Every man had his price. It was all about money, providing for your family, self-preservation, and indulging in ya desires and guilty pleasures.

The only soft spot in Frank's heart was for all the killings in Philadelphia. When he first started out, the plan was to flood the inner city with drugs, let them sell it, and get high off of it. When all the money's gone, they will rob and kill each other, then we come in and put them in jail and take everything they made for themselves. Only problem Frank has with the plan is that it's working too well. It's getting harder and harder for him to ignore all the killings. All the deaths that the pandemic caused basically wiped out our senior citizen population. The small businesses closed, and the people were out of work. The inflation, the looting, and the rioting. The fentanyl and the opioid crisis were just the beginning.

His second stop was at his favorite watering hole. An Irish pub called Micky's was located on 55th and Market Street in West Philadelphia.

Frank went to Micky's every night religiously, even if it was just to walk in for a second and speak to his buddies, but mostly it was to get drunk, smoke cigars, talk shit, and reminisce about the '80s and the '90s. Two eras where Frank honed his extortion craft and made a name for himself.

Most of the patrons who frequented there had been doing so as long as Frank and the ownership and management had been with the same family since the '60s. With Frank being a pillar and a major influence in the Irish community, Mickeys were proud to call Frank one of their own. It was his home, and he was their favorite uncle, fat, drunk, and obnoxious, always looking for a good fist fight and a cheap whore.

After clearing his old tab and starting a new one by buying everybody in the bar drinks, Frank sat there and got shit-faced for 3 hours straight. After finally feeling like he reached his perfect level of intoxication, blurred vision, disoriented and numb with a mustard seed feeling of euphoria, it was time for Frank to take his show on the road. He said his goodbyes, gave his handshakes and salutes, then staggered outside to his car.

"Where the heck are these keys at?" he mumbled as he leaned up against the driver's side car door.

He fumbled through his pants pockets for the car keys. In his drunken stupor, he didn't notice the two men approaching, both wearing black hoodies and Covid-19 masks.

"What's up, Oldhead?" one of the men asked Frank.

"You cool. What are you looking for?" the other man asked.

Frank knowing that he's well known, didn't have the slightest worry. Everybody knew he was a cop, well respected and well connected. So it would be suicide for anybody trying to rob him, and it wouldn't be the first time, but a strange feeling crept through his body and made the fine hairs on his arms rise, which cleared his drunken mind just enough for him to get a good look at one of the men.

"Chance," Frank said to himself. He was shocked, his skin turned white as if he saw a ghost. That was when reality set in because wherever Chance was, his brother Hammer wasn't but a few steps away.

Before the next thought or course of action could enter Frank's mind, he felt something cold press against the back of his head.

"BOOOOM."

The gun went off, splattering Frank's brains all over the driver's side window.

Chapter 1

August 2019

"I don't know what's up with the bull, but he acts like a nut!" Shane said to his business partner and best friend, Kirk. They were sitting in Shane's midnight blue Mercedes Benz A.M.G.

"What do you mean he's acting like a nut?" Kirk asked while looking out the passenger side window. It was pouring down, raining all day, and they were parked in the Mcdonald's parking lot on 60th and Woodland Avenue in Southwest Philadelphia.

"I don't know, I'm just getting a weird vibe from him," Shane said.

"You gave him all the money, right?" Kirk asked.

"Yeah!" Shane answered.

"All of it?" Kirk questioned with a raised eyebrow looking at Shane.

"$800,000 nigga, and I gave Maria the other $700,000 like he asked us to!" Shane answered with an attitude.

"Well, that squared us up for the last 100 bricks we got," Kirk said.

"It ain't the fucking money, Kirk. We ain't never play money games with him. I think we getting too big for him now, and he can't control us like he used to!" Shane said.

"Maybe it's because it's getting hot, like I've been telling you. Shit, I've been paranoid lately," Kirk admitted.

Shane looked at Kirk confused and said, "I don't know why! All we handle is the money now!"

"I'm just saying, it's been feeling like a little pressure around us lately," Kirk said.

"Don't start this paranoid shit, man. You always do that, Kirk. You be speaking bad things into existence on us!" Shane said.

"I be feeling the energy. You know I do!" Kirk replied.

"When was the last time we put some drugs in anybody's hand? I'm sick of ya'll niggas with this bullshit! What, you scared somebody out to rob us? Somebody is trying to kidnap one of us and hold us for ransome? What, somebody gonna try to snatch a chain when we go out to the club? We not rappers, Kirk. We move with a cartel. Our cars are armored!" Shane snapped.

"I'm talking about a R.I.C.O case," Kirk said.

"If you ain't talking about Rico from paid and full, I don't give a fuck about a Rico! We getting money and doing good. Stop by all this negative shit into my life!" Shane yelled.

Kirk shook his head in disbelief at his partner's naivety and said, "Think about it, Shane! We had a 5-

year run getting money with them. A lot of niggas would be lucky to get a run that last through the summer with out getting locked up or killed!" Kirk yelled back.

"So what's the problem, Kirk?" Shane asked.

"We should get out the game while we're ahead, Shane, while we got a chance!" Kirk answered.

Shane sat quietly for a few seconds and thought.

"Ok, let's re-up one more time then. We grab three hundred bricks of cocaine and a hundred bricks of fentanyl. After we run that off, we put a retirement plan together," Shane said.

Kirk just looks at him and smiles, knowing Shane missed the whole point. How could he get mad at Shane for not understanding that they were under a federal indictment or acting like he didn't care? He was reckless. When the F.B.I. first approached Kirk, they gave him a chance for him to save Shane, too, but Kirk knew he would never compromise.

They were friends their whole lives. Their mothers and fathers were friends. Kirk felt as though he knew Shane better than he knew himself. Shane was the life of the party, the charm and charisma that attracted the women and the money.

He came up gambling on street corners and robbing jewelry stores. Kirk came up with finessing, credit card fraud, and scamming people out of their money. He was the thinker, the organizer, and a planner but soft and timid. Whatever the case, their friendship worked, and together they flourished in the drug game, but Kirk wasn't going down for Shane's ignorance. So he made his price and sold Shane and the rest of their team to the Feds.

"You should fall back, Shane. Get low for a minute," Kirk told him.

"I need to fall back!" Shane said with a disgusted look on his face. "What the fuck you mean by I?" Shane questioned.

"You know what I'm trying to say. It ain't like we need the money. We up! We can afford to chill for a minute, go somewhere, and just live!" Kirk said.

"Man fuck that! Come on with the bullshit Kirk!" Shane said, cutting him off in the middle of what he was saying.

"How do we do that, Kirk? That shit don't even sound right. We got businesses. We wash money through them. If it ain't no money to wash, then those businesses will shut down! We got a team that depends on us to keep the work coming so they can take care of they're folks! If we fall back, you know how many niggas in the city gone fall off? It's gone. Crash the economy!" Shane finished saying.

In all honesty, Shane ain't give a fuck about them businesses, the team, or none of that shit. It was all about him. All he knew was to sell drugs and hustle. That was his life.

They had millions. They could afford to fall back, but then Shane would be out of his element, away from that lifestyle, and out of that loop was unimaginable to him. He didn't have an off switch. He was gone be lit until he got a life sentence and died in jail or died in the game by a bullet and a gun. With or without, Kirk and Kirk knew it.

Kirk wipes his hands over his face in contemplation. Three hundred bricks and a hundred bricks of fentanyl. With the feds lurking around, Kirk knew it would be hard to juggle that many at one time. They had to push them because there wouldn't be any point in sitting on them for a rainy day. They were in the eye of the storm already. A federal indictment was coming for certain. Kirk leans back in his seat. Shane already knew the answer.

"Kirk! Look at me, Kirk!" Shane said to him.

Kirk looked over at him.

"One more flip, baby. Let's make them remember us!" Shane said.

CHAPTER 2

Ya'll know what the fuck it is! Everybody stay where they at and put ya hands on top of ya fucking heads!" Chance yelled, pointing an AR15 assault rifle at six men standing around a craps table in an illegal gambling house.

"And whoever hands is not in plain sight getting shot!" Hammer yelled, approaching the men aiming a Glock 40 handgun with a switch and an extended clip.

Hammer and Chance were brothers robbing the neighborhood gambling house, the same neighborhood they grew up in and lived in.

"Ard, this how it's gone work! Whoever tries to be the hero is gone be the reason everybody dies a hero's death. All we want is the money, ya'll can keep the jewelry. That shit probably fake anyway!" Chance told the men.

"Now, one by one, I need ya'll to come over and stand right there!" Hammer said, pointing to a clear spot on the floor.

"We gon check ya'll waist for guns and money belts. We gon check ya'll pockets, ya'll take ya'll shoes off, and we gon check ya'll socks, we gon pull ya'll pants down and check to see if it's any bankrolls of money in ya'll draws. Y'all gambling mufuckas be tucking money everywhere, and we want it all!" Chance said.

"And anybody who does anything other than what we said is getting dropped. You gone get posted on Nogunzone, I promise. First one up, let's go playa!" Hammer said, leading one of the men to the designated spot and checking him while Chance held the other men at bay with the assault rifle.

By the time they were done with the fifth person, they had found two money belts, three guns, and tens of thousands of dollars.

"Ard, come on, pimp, let's go!" Hammer said to the last guy, the manager of the gambling house.

He started walking towards the spot but then stopped and said, "I wasn't gonna say anything. I was just going to charge it to the game. Put a bag on ya'll head and send somebody to drop ya'll later, but ya'll must have lost yall mind. What the fuck ya'll niggas high off? Ya'll don't know who the fuck we are, who the fuck I am?" The manager said, voice getting louder and growing confidence with every word he spoke.

Hammer raised the gun to slap him across the face with it, but Chance stopped him.

"Who are you?" Chance asked the man.

"My name Jax, Youngbull!" The man said with a voice full of pride, looking over at the other men for their co-sign.

Even though Hammer and Chance recognized his name it, didn't matter to them. They had no picks. You couldn't reason with a hungry wolf.

"Yeah, I heard of you!" Chance said.

"I know ya'll Youngbulls, ya'll live around the corner," Jax told them. "Ya'll think ya'll gon get away with this. I know you're hungry, but you bit off more than you can chew with this one!" Jax said.

"Keep ya money then, Oldhead, I'll take ya life instead!" Hammer said before he shot him in the face, brain matter, blood, and bone fragments flew out the back of his head and showered the other men close to him. They just watched as his lifeless body crumpled to the floor.

"Anybody else feel like expressing themselves and the need to let us know who you are?" Hammer asked the other men. They all kept quiet.

"Take the keys out of his pocket and hit the safe!" Chance told Hammer.

* * *

"$167,815!" Hammer said to Chance, now inside their godmother's house at the dining room table, wrapping the money in rubber bands.

"All we really up is $60,000. We owe John John $80,000, and I gotta give Mama Meechie that $27,000 we lost at the casino last night." Chance said.

"You talking about the $27,000 you lost at the casino last night!" Hammer responded.

"You was right there with me nigga!" Chance said.

"I was with you, but I ain't shake or roll, not one pair of dice. That was all ya work, playa!" Hammer said.

"So you wasn't trying to coach my bets? Put another $500 on the 6, put $1,000 on the 8, double down on the 9. They were ya bets. I was just rolling the dice!" Chance said.

"Fuck outa here! You was in heat, and I was just trying to help you win ya money back, but once you lost that first ten grand, I knew you was gone lose everything!" Hammer countered.

"It's ya bad energy. You be thinking I'm a loose that's why I lose. Instead of thinking ima win so I can win. You a bad gambling partner, brother, straight up!" Chance said.

"You keep forgetting I don't gamble. I'll just be there in case I gotta shoot somebody or we gotta rob somebody after you lose all the money!" Hammer reminded him.

"What about when me and Oldhead Duke was gambling, and I won $15,000 from him?" Chance asked.

"We spent $5,000 on clothes, and that same night you lost the other $10,000 plus the $4,000 we had in the house!" Hammer said, looking at Chance like he was crazy.

"You a hater," Chance said.

"Now I'm a hater. You are not a gambler. If you ain't have bad luck, you wouldn't have no luck. You a hustla, and I'm a shooter. That's what it is! Every time we get some work, you gamble the money away, then we gotta go take it back!" Hammer said.

It was the truth. Chance was a bad gambler. No matter how many times or how much money he lost, he believed the next time he went to gamble, he would break the house. His model was that you lose more than you win, but when you win, you win big. Even though what Hammer said to him stung, he didn't get mad. It wasn't the first time.

"I ain't trying to hear that shit, brother. Let's just get the money together!" Chance said.

* * *

Their godmother's name was Demetrius, "Mama Meechie" Douglas. She was a 65-year-old recovered drug addict and had been living in Southwest Philadelphia her whole life.

Throughout her years of getting high, all of her children were taken from her by the Department Of Human Services and placed in foster homes or put up for adoption. Some were taken right out of her arms after she birthed them because of complications and side effects from being exposed to crack cocaine and alcohol while in her womb.

Meechie had been clean for 20 years now. From day one of her sobriety, she devoted herself to the children in her neighborhood with mothers who are heavy in their addiction like she used to be. It was a way for her to deal with the extreme anguish and guilt she felt for losing her kids and all the awful things she did in her life. She started a nonprofit called "They Care Demetrius."

She didn't have much money except for the small private donations she received. She fed, clothed, and sheltered whoever she could, whenever she could. What she had the most to offer out of everything was loving, kind, and encouraging words and advice whenever someone needed it. She was deemed the neighborhood's godmother, and her home became a safe haven.

She understood the kids and their problems. She didn't judge them for the way they were or how they turned out to be: drug dealers, robbers, killers, and some even drug addicts themselves. Most of the kids she took in ended up dead, in prison, or still running the streets in another part of the city, state, or country.

The local police and the district attorney tried to demonize her by saying, "She is a corrupt woman with a corrupt organization that takes kids off the streets and groom them to be better drug dealers, robbers, and killers, and she's paid a percentage of their profits." Whether the allegations are true or not it's up for debate, and it depends on who you are debating with.

What they never noticed or mentioned about Mama Meechie was the few kids that she helped get into college, get jobs, buy homes and start families. Society condemned her, but the hood held her in high esteem.

Out of her 20 years of community service, she had a few favorites, and they were called her Meechie Boys. Hammer and Chance now carried around that title. Mother and Father dead, abandoned before their teens. She was the only family they had.

* * *

"What are we doing tonight, Chance?" Hammer asked after they finished counting and putting rubber bands around the rolls of money.

"We owe Mack 80k, right?" Chance asked Hammer.

"Yeah," he answered.

"We gotta score. We can't burn them niggas. Mufuckas are already scared to serve us cause we be robbing and drilling. Give Meechie her money and give her this 20 to put up for us," Chance told Hammer.

"So we giving her 50 altogether?" Hammer asked.

"Yeah, an extra three thousand for her. That leaves us with $37,000 after we re-up!" Chance said.

"Let's go to Philly Auto and see if they let us trade the car in with some money for something new," Hammer said.

"We can do that, then go shopping at K.O.P and get fresh. Hit the club tonight and fuck with some bitches!" Chance said.

"That's the move!" Hammer replied.

Chapter 3

"Why do we have to sit here surveillance this old man at this busted down used car lot?" asked Frank's new partner Alfonso Cruz. Now in his second year of the narcotics division.

"You don't ever stop asking questions, do you? Instead of just sitting here and being observant, all you do is run your mouth!" Frank snapped, now at his tipping point.

Every day for the last six weeks since they were first paired up, all Alfonso did was ask questions and talk, From the beginning to the end of the shift, and Frank couldn't take it anymore.

"I'm tired of hearing you nag and complain! Your worst than my second wife, for the love of god. Just shut the fuck up!" Frank yelled.

Frank smacked the dashboard of his unmarked police vehicle, knocking over a cup of coffee from the cup holder.

"Fuck! Fuck! Fuck!" Frank screamed as the steaming coffee spilled on his leg. He grabbed some napkins and tried to clean up the mess.

Alfonso struggled to hold in his laughter before pointing his finger at Frank and saying, “Look here, I’ma grown man Frank, and you are not gon’ be talking to me in that manner. I don’t want to be around you just as much as you don’t want to be around me. I didn’t ask to be put in your company!”

Frank stared at him and takes a deep breath trying to hold his composure. He felt the sweat building on the back of his neck and dripping down his spine. He already had a massive headache from a long night of drinking, and the pitch of Alfonso’s voice was making it worse. He could feel his blood pressure building in the back of his eyeballs and threatening to pop them right out of the socket.

Throughout his entire career, Frank only had six partners, all people he chose, all men of his caliber. All men that somewhat understood the streets knew the etiquette of a police officer and knew the lines and boundaries to cross and not to cross.

Frank knew that the department just paired him with this new boot to keep an eye on him and disrupt his flow, and he wouldn’t be surprised if Alfonso was with internal affairs investigating some of the allegations, trying to bust him and ruin his legacy.

“All I’m saying is that since we are forced to work together, for however long, that might be, can we try to make the best of it?” Alfonso continued.

Frank took another deep breath. Not paying attention to anything that the kid is saying. A so-called veteran to rookies program, a bunch of bullshit, Frank felt.

When he was making his way through the police ranks, it wasn't all this buddy-buddy shit. You didn't ask too many questions, and you figured it out on your own. You pulled yourself up by your own bootstraps, and either a joker was cut out to be one of Philadelphia's finest, or he wasn't. Bottom line.

"And I don't mind surveillance, Frank. I just would like to be informed on what we are surveilling. Informed on the assignment for the day so I can be prepared, and know what to expect, Frank! I don't like sitting around or riding around and not knowing anything!" Alfonso continued.

It took everything in Franks' will not to drive off to a secluded park, tell the kid to get out and grab something from behind a tree and shoot him dead.

"Are you listening to me, Frank?" Alfonso asked.

"Look, kid, if you could please be quiet and let me concentrate on the cars coming in and out of this lot when we leave, I'll inform you on the purpose of all of it!" Frank pleaded.

"Alright, Frank!" Alfonso said, leaning back in his seat, somewhat satisfied.

In all actuality, Alfonso wasn't as green as Frank thought. He was born and raised in Philadelphia, a section of the city called the Badlands, which was dominated by Hispanics. Everything went on in the Badlands, and Alfonso was exposed to it all at one point or another. From drug dealing, murder, rap, extortion, kidnapping, you name it. The Badlands was like a small city inside the city where outsiders were not welcomed.

Alfonso was 28 years old and had a little sister named Rebecca, who was 23 and still in college. Their father, Hector Cruz, died of a heroin overdose when Alfonso was seven years old, and his mother, Sonia Cruz, met the same fate a year later. Alfonso and his sister were placed in D.H.S. custody for a few months, and after some legal formalities, their grandparents were awarded custody of them.

The death of their parents wasn't really a change for Alfonso and Rebecca because their grandparents basically had them since birth anyway. Whenever the mom and dad went on their drug binges, the kids were left with the grandparents for weeks at a time, and there were very few sober days between them. The mom and dad basically became friends of the family who came over every once in a while, to take them to the store to buy candy, nothing more. All their love was for their grandparents.

Sonia was a loving grandmother and a very religious and spiritual person. She took Alfonso and Rebecca to church every Sunday and to bible study every Monday, Wednesday, and Friday. Sonia took advantage of all the social service programs that the church and community had to offer. The clothing drives, the food drives, the after-school programs, and activities. They went on every field trip and volunteered every time community service was needed at the church.

Jose was a stern grandfather, the provider. He worked 12-hour shifts at a fruit packing factory five days out of the week. On his off days, he spent as much time with Alfonso as he could. He knew how important it was for him to have someone positive to look up to. If not, he would find a false positive in the streets. Jose vowed not to make the same mistakes with Alfonso that he made with Hector.

Jose made sure he instilled principles in him and tried to ground him in morals and values as much as he could. Teach him how to be a confident, respected, responsible man. Teach him that life had more to offer and the world was much bigger than the confines of the Badlands. In return, Alfonso and Rebecca built a solid understanding of good and bad, right from wrong. Despite being surrounded by the evils of a drug-riddled neighborhood, they stayed away from the streets and the fast life and focused on their studies, and excelled in school.

In middle school, Alfonso had a growth spurt. He went from 5’8 to 6’2 almost overnight. With his new height, he was pressured into sports. First, he tried basketball, but he failed miserably, then baseball, then he finally tried football and found his calling as a special team’s kicker for his high school.

All those years of playing soccer in the church yard paid off. His leg was so strong he could kick a 50-

yard field goal in the 10th grade. He was a phenomenon and was given a scholarship and recruited by the University of Penn State. He was a Nittany lion. A dream came true for him, his entire family, and the church congregation.

In his freshman year, he played in only three games. The starting kicker pulled a hamstring giving Alfonso his shot. He performed well but didn't live up to the expectations, but the coaching staff believed in him, and he was promised to start his junior year, and he did.

The Sunday following his fourth game of the new season, he got a call from the Philadelphia homicide division saying that it was very important that he came back to Philadelphia to speak with them immediately.

Alfonso was informed that one evening his grandparents heard a commotion in front of their house. They peeked out the window to see what was going on and witnessed a young man get shot to death right in front of their eyes. Being that it was right in front of their house when the police showed up, they knocked on their door to see if they saw anything. They were both taken to the police station and questioned. They both gave statements and descriptions of what they saw, which ultimately led to the police making an arrest. The suspect arrested was the nephew of the biggest drug dealer in the Badlands.

Rebecca begged and pleaded for them not to cooperate with the police, but Sonia couldn't sit back and let an animal roam the streets like that, possibly kill again in cold blood. When word got out that Sonia and Hose were snitching, a hit was put on them.

Saturday morning, the day of Alfonso's fourth game, someone broke into Maria and Jose's house and shot them both to death while they lay in bed asleep. Then the house was doused in gasoline and set on fire. Fortunately, Rebecca was at her girlfriend's house for a sleepover.

Alfonso was devastated. He quit playing football, lost his scholarship, and dropped out of school. Alfonso became an alcoholic and contemplated suicide every waking morning until his eyes shut again at night.

With the life insurance policy from their grandparents, Rebecca was able to go to college and pursue a career. To get her mind off of what happened to her grandparents, She buried herself in schoolwork. She had no time to think of anything else, not even Alfonso.

After a few years of deep depression and soul searching, Alfonso finally got himself together and off the booze. He knew what his new mission in life was, to catch and help prosecute the criminals and gangstas like the ones that took his grandparents from him. He became a cop, an overly ambitious and aggressive cop with a chip on his shoulder. To him, whoever didn't stand with or behind the law, was against the law. Everybody without a badge was assumed to be a criminal until proven otherwise.

* * *

After 45 minutes of silence, Frank scribbled down 4 license plate numbers and descriptions of the vehicles and drivers. That was enough for the day. It was time to roll. Once he got some privacy, he would run the tag numbers and see who the vehicles were registered to. Maybe he would find something interesting enough to give credence to his suspicions.

"Where are we headed now, Frank?" Alfonso asked after Franked pulled out of the parking spot and headed up the street. Frank just ignored him and kept driving.

CHAPTER 4

"Yo Kirk, where the fuck is all the other money machines? You know how long it's gone take to count all this with just two of these mufuckas!" Shane said to Kirk.

They were at one of their stash houses in Montgomery County, Pennsylvania.

"John John on his way with the other 4," Kirk said.

"Why the fuck John got them? Why he don't he have his own?" Shane questioned Kirk.

Kirk shrugged his shoulders.

"Never in my life would I have ever imagined the hardest and most stressful part of my day would be counting and bagging up $11 million dollars! Can you believe this, Kirk? How many mufuckas do you know that wish they could pay somebody to count their money?" Shane asked Kirk.

They were getting their re-up money together.

"You are the only person I know, playa!" Kirk answered while running more money through the machine, then punching the number count in his calculator then adding that number to the total in his little black notebook.

"But on some real shit, it's harder than it might seem. I'm not gonna lie," Kirk added.

"You goddamn right! I figured it might start getting easier after you've been getting money for so long, but this shit in the way!" Shane said.

Kirk nodded in agreement.

Shane got up off the living room couch, went into the kitchen, and came back with a bottle of Bottega champagne. He popped the cork then, guzzled it and flopped back down on the couch.

"Ahhhhh, I need a drink. Get my nerves together!" Shane said.

Kirk shook his head at him and finished counting the money.

"This is like a full-time job, Kirk! Count it, separate it by denominations, bag it up, and stash it. You can't even say fuck it and let the money pile up and do it all on one day because you gone be doing that it for days!" Shane said.

"Plus, you don't want bags of money laying around all over the place!" Kirk added.

"I wish they would come out with $1,000 bills, 5,000- and 10,000-dollar bills. That would make this process way faster and smoother, right? Shane asked.

Kirk ignored him.

"Remember when we first met the line?" Shane then asked.

"Yeah," Kirk answered.

"We thought that nigga was frauding, talking bout he the plug in the city. I was like, if you don't get ya nut ass outta here, Oldhead!" Shane said.

"Till he put that brick of fish scale in our face!" Kirk said.

"I couldn't believe it. I swore he was trying to line us up for the feds or something, remember?" Shane asked Kirk.

"Yeah, we was fucked up, grabbing half ounces and 62s!" Kirk answered.

"Remember we thought the coke was fake because how it swelled up in the pot when we dropped it in the water?" Shane asked.

"Never seen coke like that before!" Kirk answered.

Shane tries to hand Kirk the bottle again, but he denies it again, this time by holding his hand up and shaking his head no. Shane flops back down on the couch and takes another sip.

"It feels like another lifetime ago," Kirk said.

"Remember he gave us that nut-ass speech about loyalty and all that bullshit?" Shane asked.

"Yeah, I remember!" Kirk said, standing up from the dining room table, stretching his back, then sitting back down to finish.

"Yo, he swears he the wisest mufucka in the world, think he got all the game! Scary ass Oldhead!" Shane said.

"Shit, he changed our lives like he said he was gone do. We both would probably be broke, dead, or in jail by now if it wasn't for him. Cautious, that's the word to describe him, not scary. How do you think he lasted this long?" Kirk asked Shane.

Shane balled his face up with an attitude like he was just insulted and said, "You probably would of been broke, dead, or in jail nigga! Me!"

Shane stood up from the couch and pointed to his chest for emphasis. "Me! I'll still be getting money right now if we never met him. Broke is not a trait that runs in my family, D.N.A. pimp!"

Kirk chuckled to himself, knowing Shane was just arrogant and full of shit. Kirk figured he might as well push his buttons a lil' bit, get a few laughs.

"Now, don't get me wrong, it might have taken us a lil' bit longer to get to the level we are at now if it wasn't for Oldhead, but we would have eventually found a line and been on our way!" Shane stated as a matter of fact.

"Yeah, that little half of brick we were flipping was gone. Get us there!" Kirk said in a joking manner.

"We was stacking our money tho nigga, and we was where we was supposed to be for just getting in the game! You're taking credit away from our hustle. How are you gonna do that?" Shane asked.

Kirk smiled, knowing he got him where he wanted him.

"How many niggas we met that said all they needed was for somebody to put them on?" Shane asked, then sipped from the bottle before he continued talking.

"We throw them niggas a brick of fish scale, and they ain't even got mufucka they can sell a gram to and end up fucking the money up. Niggas want to be bosses but don't even know how to be a boss. They want all the bricks but don't even know how to manufacture them. They can't cook, cut, or compress when needed. Can't weed out the real get-money niggas from the frauds. Can't manage the money, manage the clientele, can't manage the trap. It's more than just having the work, baby, you know that. It's the hustle behind the work!" Shane said.

Kirk laughed.

"Why the fuck is you always laughing nigga!" Shane snapped.

"All that slick shit you talking, manage the money, manage the trap. Let me see you do that shit with a 100 bricks of bullshit!" Kirk said.

Shane stared at him for a second, then smiled before saying, "I know what you doing, Kirk. You just tryna hear me talk my shit! I wish I knew how to rap. I'll make a album, so whenever you need to hear a real nigga speak, you can just listen to it!" Shane said.

"Fuck outa here!" Kirk said.

Shane sits back down on the couch and sips from the bottle again before saying, "When you gone get with

Oldhead cause I don't feel like dealing with that nigga this time. All that weird shit turning me off!"

"Once we get the money right, pack it in the car and get it to the drop spot, I'ma hit him up. That way, he can just scoop the bread and let us know when and where to pick the work up!" Kirk answered.

"What are John and Shorty in the books for?" Shane asked.

"John John $600,000, he bringing $500,000 with him," Kirk answered, then looked through one of his lil' black notebooks on the dining room table.

He scrolled down a page with his index finger until he found what he was looking for. "Shorty, $250,000, but he got three more days to turn over!" Kirk said.

"Ard, I wish this nigga hurry up with them money machines so we can get this over with. I got something to do tonight!" Shane said.

"You might as well come help, keep the count or something," Kirk suggested.

"I don't count money by hand, no more, baby. That's what the money machines are for!" Shane said.

CHAPTER 5

It was 2:30 a.m. Hammer and Chance had just left a nightclub on Delaware Avenue after a long night of partying and drinking. They had two girls with them, Carmen and Angela, two bottles of Ciroc, and an ounce of some Runtz weed. They were at the Marriott Hotel in Southwest Philadelphia by the airport.

"Go ahead and drink, shorty, don't get shy now! Chance said to Carmen, handing her the bottle.

"You know ain't nobody shy, boy!" Carmen said, grabbing the bottle from Chance and taking a healthy sip.

They were in the lounge area of the indoor pool. They had no swim trunks or bikinis. Chance and Hammer were in their boxers. Carmen and Angela were in their panties and bras. Usually, the pool was closed this time of night, but Chance threw the manager a couple of dollars to let them in.

"Stand up baby, let me see what ya body look like. You took ya clothes off so fast and sat down I didn't even get a chance to admire you!" Chance said to Carmen.

Carmen smiled. Her little bashful act was all a game. She liked to be chased and seduced a little bit. See how bad they want it, then see how much money she can finesse out of them. She knew what she had and what to do with it.

She stood up and backed away from the table she was sitting on. She bit her bottom lip seductively as she looked at Chance. She stood on her tippy toes, and poked her ass out so he could get a good look at how fat her pussy was between the gap in her legs. Then she spun around slowly so he could get a 360 view of her body and all her curves.

Carmen stood at 5'7, with honey-brown skin, almond-shaped eyes, and a luscious set of lips that were made for kissing and sucking dick. She had a nice plump apple bottom ass and a pair of double-D cup titties to compliment it. She had a long black silky lace front weave that was pulled back into a loose pony tail to show off the diamond studs in her earlobes. Her fingernails and toes were french manicured, and her kneecaps weren't 5 shades darker than the rest of her body which meant she didn't kneel in front of every man she faced. She was a fancy whore.

They say the devil is in the details, and one thing Chance did was pay attention to them. So after sizing Carmen up, he got a lil' nervous because some would say she was an arm's length out of his reach, but he pulled her. Which let him know that arm's length was cut down to a few fingers.

He and Hammer reached another level of the game. They were climbing.

He smiled at the thought of it, grabbed the bottle, and took a long sip.

"You like what you see, Daddy?" Carmen asked Chance after sitting back down, noticing the change in his demeanor. She thought it was lust, but it was much more.

"I love it, baby. Come sit on my lap. Let me tell you something in ya ear," Chance said to her.

"Yes, Daddy," Carmen replied, getting up and walking her sexy ass over to Chance and sitting in his lap.

Hammer was hugged up with Angela inside the pool, who was equally as bad as Carmen but of a lighter complexion.

Chance was socially conscious. He liked being popular. Even though he was a drug dealer, robber, and killer, it was a certain level of sophistication and class he carried himself with. He knew how to hold his tongue, think before he spoke and be polite when he needed to be. He knew about diplomacy. He could be laughing and joking with a person one minute while plotting to kill him the next minute. He cared about what people thought, cared about opinions, and challenged anybody who thought less of what he and Hammer thought of themselves.

Hammer was the total opposite of Chance. He didn't give a fuck what nobody had to say except

Chance. A person could think whatever they wanted, but if somebody disrespected him or Chance in any way, shape, or form, they were dead. If something of that nature was brought to his attention, he would find the source and down them.

He never cared about fitting in, never cared about being a boss or a fly nigga, if he was liked or disliked. He never cared about a bad bitch or a nasty attitude because if he couldn't pull her off G, he tricked her. If she wasn't tricking, he would find a bitch that was. Everything looked like a nail to him. That was why they called him Hammer.

"You gonna rip 'em," Angela said to Hammer, who was pulling her panties off.

They were now in their hotel room. Chance was in the other room with Carmen.

"If I rip 'em, I'll buy you some more!" Hammer said, now pulling her panties from around her ankles while she lay on the bed giggling.

"Why do they call you Hammer?" she asked.

"You're about to find out!" he answered while stepping out of his boxers, dick already hard. The only thing on his mind was pounding. No kissing, no hugging, no caressing, just hard fucking.

He grabbed her legs and flipped her over on her stomach, then grabbed her by her hips and pulled her to the edge of the bed where he was standing so she was in the doggy-style position. Without another word, he went into her raw and answered her question.

* * *

The next morning Chance woke up to his cell phone ringing and the worst headache of his life. Carmen was still sleeping, naked on her stomach in between his legs. She was riding Chance, reverse cowgirl, and after they both nutted, she rose off his dick and collapsed where she lay. Chance did the same.

Chance reached for his cell phone with one hand while rubbing Carmen's fat ass with his other hand.

"Yooo!" Chance said into the phone.

"You ain't dressed and ready yet nigga! Hammer yelled, his voice sounding like a loud speaker in Chance's ear. "I'm in the parking lot. Come on, we out!" Hammer finished, then hung up the phone.

Chance lay there for a minute, looking at Carmen's gorgeous body while she slept. He thought about getting on top of her and sliding in, waking her up with a stiff dick, but he never minded it. She had his number. He knew he would see her again. If not, he knew it was better bitches to come.

He pulled his legs from under her and got dressed without waking her. He left $250 on the night stand by her purse, then left.

Hammer was sitting in the parking lot with the car running, an all-black 2017 Audi S5. Hammer got a system put in it, tinted windows, black headlights, and rear lights, then lifted the frame a couple of inches so he could put black rims on it. Chance could hear the base banging while he approached the car.

"Glock 40 on my hip, cop killers in the clip, state troopers pull us over! I'm killing him on the shoulder! Blowwww! nigga, right in his face. I rather catch a body then get caught with all this weight! If I catch a fed case, I'm getting life anyway! So why not take a life to try and get away? Unh! I'm from Philadelphia, Pa., where niggas ride for less, niggas die for less! Kill you for respect or that chain around ya neck! Just to run around and brag about it in the projects!"

A song called "Respect" from a Philadelphia rapper named Cuddy came blaring out the speakers when Chance opened the car door and hopped in.

"Always tryna lay up. I bet you gave her some money, too, didn't you?" Hammer questioned after turning the music down.

"Fuck outa here," Chance replied, leaning his seat back.

"I know you did. That's why I robbed her girlfriend while she was asleep!" Hammer said.

Chance glanced at him and closed his eyes, his headache too severe to spar with him.

"The bitch only had $40 in her purse, probably from the last nigga she fucked. I found these, though!"

Hammer held his hand out, showing 6 Percocet pills.

Chance tried to snatch them all but could only get 4. He threw them in his mouth before Hammer could protest.

"I needed them mufuckas, brother, my head pounding!" Chance said while Hammer threw the other 2 pills in his mouth.

"John John in Southwest, he said meet him at the gas station on 52nd and Woodland Avenue," Hammer told Chance.

"We gotta grab the money from Mama crib," Chance said.

"I just came from there. You know I don't sleep!" Hammer handed Chance a Walmart bag with $80,000 in it.

"Cool, where the weed at? You ain't roll nothing up?" Chance asked Hammer.

"That's the passenger job nigga. I'm pushing the A-5 today!" Hammer told Chance.

He put the car in reverse, backed out of the parking spot, and pulled off.

Chance went into the glovebox, pulled out a sandwich bag full of weed and a pack of backwoods, then rolled a blunt up while Hammer drove.

"Now this nigga want to be coming to Southwest! He a Northeast bull, When he start doing that?" Chance questioned.

"He probably got another trap around here!" Hammer answered.

"Yeah, probably," Chase said. Then got quiet for a second, thinking.

"Fuck you thinking bout nigga?" Hammer asked.

"I don't know. It just seems like everybody moving different. You can't tell?" Chance asked.

"All these niggas move like pussies to me!" Hammer said, shrugging.

"It feel like people moving in position or something! Like when you play chess and bull just slides his rook or his queen down the board to see what you do!" Chance said, then lit the weed and took a deep puff.

"Man, who the fuck thinking about chess?" Hammer asked, looking at him confused.

Chance let out a cloud of smoke from his lungs through his nostrils, then coughed. "Wooooo!" he said as he tried to catch his breath.

"This some fucking gas nigga! You high! Pass the bud nigga!" Hammer said, swerving the car through traffic and looking over at him.

Chance took another puff and then passed it to him.

Hammer grabbed the blunt and looked at it before taking a puff, then looked back at the road swerving back into his lane of traffic.

When they pulled into the gas station, they saw John John's silver and black custom F250 Ford pickup truck. Hammer slid into a parking spot. Chance grabbed the Walmart bag and tucked it in his hoodie pocket.

"This fat nigga probably sitting in his truck with a Bucket of chicken, Biscuits, and gravy early in the fucking morning!" Chance joked.

Hammer laughed.

"Sit tight," Chance said, then hopped out of the car to score from John John.

CHAPTER 6

Alfonso sat at his desk in the narcotics division and inconspicuously glanced across the room at Frank, who had a phone pressed between his hairy ear and shoulder, talking to someone while tapping on his computer with two fat Vienna sausage-looking fingers.

Alfonso was sure Frank was up to something no good. Why else would he be so sensitive about his work? The only time an officer of the law went through extreme measures to be private was to hide something he didn't want exposed. If it was good, why hide it?

Alfonso looked around the room and wondered what the other detectives thought about Frank's weird demeanor and if maybe some of them were in cahoots with him or maybe Frank's highly decorated career and arrogant, snobby attitude intimidated everyone else, so they minded their own business. Whatever the case was, he would never ask them. It was too close to home.

Alfonso knew about Frank's connections and wasn't ignorant of the rumors but had no reason to believe them. Even now, with Frank acting the way he was, some of these rumors were a far stretch. If it was even a lil' bit of truth to them, it would make Frank no better than the criminals they pursued. He was sure the other cops had to do their due diligence to make sure they weren't true. If not, it would compromise the integrity of the whole department. How many criminals that were on Frank's case load would get new trials and possibly be set free?

Then again, maybe some of the other detectives were involved, did a little damage control, and Frank's connections helped his dirt get swept under a rug. If Frank went down, how many other people could he bring down with him? He definitely didn't seem like a guy that would go down without a fight. That would bring in Internal affairs, the F.B.I., major indictment. It would be a disgrace to the city, the police force, and everything it stood for. So they had to protect Frank.

Then Alfonso thought that maybe he was tripping and his imagination was getting the best of him, but what if he was right? He didn't know. His grandfather always told him to follow his instincts. What did he have to lose, a friendship that was one-sided because Frank clearly didn't like him? Dirty looks from other cops because he helped bring down some of his own. Alfonso didn't care because the dirty cops weren't of his own.

He was straight-laced. When he took that oath and swore to serve and protect, he meant it. How could he turn a blind eye and go against everything his grandparents taught him? So he figured he might as well keep up his game of annoying rookie cop with the questions and the talking since it bothered Frank so much. He could use that to chip and chip away at Frank's armor until he finally got him to open up or to throw him off balance, and he stepped off his square just enough for Alfonso to get a foot on it.

"Yea, I'm reading it now! I know who she is. I've seen her before!" Frank said into the phone and then typed something into the computer.

"I wasn't aware of that. That's now!" he said, then wrote something in his notebook. He then exited what he was looking at on the computer screen.

"Can't we talk about it tonight, for Christ sake?" Frank asked the person on the other end of the phone.

"Yea, Mickey's! Alright, see ya there!" Frank hung up the call, and as much as he tried, he couldn't stop the smirk from creeping across his face until he looked over and saw Alfonso staring at him.

Frank wondered what his problem was. He caught the little prick stealing glances at him from across the room. He never knew a person so noisy and annoying in his life. He had one thing on his agenda for the day. Plant a GPS tracking device under somebody's car and find out the schedule and the locations where they frequent. That was it. He could track them on his phone or off his computer. The only problem was planting the tracking device without Alfonso knowing.

Then he thought, what if somebody recognized him while he was planting it and let the person know he was snooping around their car? Everybody who was somebody knew who Frank was. He was sure he would be spotted, and the plan would be ruined.

He figured maybe he could get Alfonso to plant it. Just make up a bogus story about it. Shit, that might be the answer to his problems for the little prick. Use him as a flunky since he wants to be so involved, and just lie to him about the reason and the purpose behind his work. So if a rumor was to start off some of it, he would know that Alfonso was the source. If it turned out that Alfonso was trustworthy and could keep a secret 'for the greater good' as Frank would put it, better than he could keep his opinions and comments to himself, Frank could possibly use him as a runner.

Frank stood up and waved to get Alfonso's attention. "Come on, kid, let's roll!" he said.

Alfonso was surprised and skeptical at the same time about the change in Frank's voice and demeanor. This was the first time Frank engaged him that way. Maybe Frank was turning around, Alfonso thought, probably tired of being a dick head and ready to involve him so they could get quality police work done. Arrest some bad guys. Maybe this was the brake he needed. Alfonso told himself to hope for the best and expect the worst. The ball was on Frank's court now.

"You got it, sir!" Alfonso said, jumping up and following Frank out the door.

"So run this by me one more time!" Alfonso said to Frank.

They were now sitting in a marked police car on 26th and Garrett Street in South Philadelphia.

"This guy is a suspected meth dealer for a pagan motorcycle club called 'Hell's Chair,' and supposedly from an inside source I have, they are getting ready to make a huge deal," Frank said, already starting to forget the lie he put together.

"I've been investigating these sons of bitches for months, and this might be our chance to finally get a solid bust and land some hard evidence that could hopefully bring down a federal indictment on the whole chapter of the club. We need this!" Frank added enthusiastically.

Frank help up the GPS for the second time.

"Right!" Alfonso said, looking at it and nodding to Frank's story while comparing it to the first story he told.

"We need this GPS planted under that forest green Suburban that's parked at the top of the block," Frank said.

Frank paused for a moment, hoping he didn't forget anything he said from the first story. Alfonso just looked at him with a raised eyebrow, edging him to continue.

"Right!" Frank said, then paused again, forgetting where he had left off. "Oh yea, so hopefully, we find a new address he frequents the most, set up a little surveillance to see who comes and goes. Try to find enough probable cause to get a few wire taps, hopefully, a few search warrants!"

Frank eyed Alfonso to see if he was falling for it.

"All right, Frank, let's do it!" Alfonso held his hands out.

Frank dropped the GPS in his palm, and Alfonso hopped out of the car and headed up the street.

"He must really think I'ma fool!" Alfonso said to himself while he casually walked up the block to carry out his task.

Pagan motorcycle club and one of its members was parked in this part of South Philly. It was nothing but Black people around here, weed, crack, and heroin. A pagan had no business being parked around here. Cops rarely rode through or parked around here. Alfonso felt like his intelligence as a narcotic detective was being insulted to the 10th power.

He knew it was all a crock of shit, and Frank was lying because he couldn't even look him in the eyes. A man of Frank's nature had no problem looking a man in the eyes when he spoke to him, especially if he was telling the truth. All the pausing was him trying to remember the lie he had told.

Then Alfonso figured it was probably a test from Frank, just to see if he could hold his tongue and not run his mouth. A test he would pass, even though it belittled him and made him feel foolish. He told himself to suck it up and looked at it as an initiation to gain Frank's trust because if Frank had to go through this to conceal his intentions, then he had to be up to something illegal or close to it.

Then he came up with an idea. He glanced at the license plate number on the suburban and remembered it. He had a favor down at the D.M.V. so he could find out who it was registered to, and he knew it wasn't gonna be a pagan. He didn't want to use a police dispatcher in case it got back to Frank, so yea. He figured the D.M.V. would be perfect.

Once he found out that the Suburban had nothing to do with a motorcycle club, he could come up with a countermeasure to watch Frank, and whoever Frank was watching. Beat Frank to the punch, and let him walk right into the blitz.

He bent down like he was tying his shoe and placed the GPS in the wheel well of the tire. He looked at the license plate and locked it in his memory, and casually walked back to the unmarked car and got in.

"Good job, kid," Frank said.

"Yes, sir!" Alfonso responded.

CHAPTER 7

"First of all, I want to thank everybody who came out to enjoy this lovely night and celebrate with us!" Shane said to a crowd of party goers at the grand opening of a new night club called 'The sky lounge.' Kirk was on stage beside him, as well as two business partners of Shane and Kirk.

"For everybody who knows me, ya'll know how I talk and mean no harm by the way I choose my words. With that being said, it's some bad bitches in here tonight!" Shane said.

The men in the crowd start to whistle and clap, and the bitches started to blush and giggle at the comment.

"Got dam, I see you, baby," Shane said to a pretty redbone woman, wearing next to nothing draped in diamonds. "I'm serious. Philadelphia and the Tri-State area got the baddest bitches on the east coast, hands down! I know it's some Florida, Atlanta, a couple from the Carolinas, the D.M.V. and New York bitches in here too, don't get me wrong cause y'all bitches bad, but my bitches representing tonight!" he added.

Kirk chuckled to himself and shook his head. Shane never relinquished the spotlight, and the crowd seemed to be enjoying him as well and kept cheering him on.

"I ain't gon hold y'all for too long," Shane continues. "I just want to remind everybody and inform the ones here tonight that have never been to a Shane and Kirk's party that no wallet and purses are needed. As you can see, all the cheap drinks have been removed. It's only top shelf, and we got cases and cases. The bar is open. It's free all night, so drink till your heart's content. Please don't be shy and help ya self," Shane finished.

He looked over at Kirk, and Kirk stepped up to speak.

"The grills are open, it's a menu up in the back, and there will be a waiter walking around to take orders. So please enjoy the food. We got a few special invited guests. The DJ will make the announcements as they arrive! Oh, yea, there's photographers and videographers here to document this affair, so if anybody would like pictures or a DVD, leave a p.o box or e-mail address, and they'll be sent personally!" Kirk said.

"And one more thing," Shane cut in. "The theme of this celebration is called The Last Run, so let's party carefree tonight like it's the last one!"

With that being said, the DJ began to play music, and the bar was flooded. Bottles of all the top-shelf liquor, wine, and champagne were passed out and poured into cups. The women got loose once the alcohol started to run through their veins, and they hit the dance floor. The men followed.

In no time, the celebration was in full swing. Everybody who was somebody within a 100-mile radius was there to show off the latest fashions, the newest cars, and the clearest diamonds.

Shane and Kirk walked off the back of the stage and took a secret exit and staircase to a private suite/office on the second floor. The walls of the suite were laced with silk wallpaper. In the middle of the living room, built into the floor, was a huge piece of translucent glass so you could look down into the club at the dance floor, but they couldn't look up and see you. They only could see themselves in the mirror.

Plush oriental rugs hugged the rest of the floor. Crystal chandeliers hung from the ceiling and sparkled like diamonds. The furniture was made out of cherry wood and black leather. They had a fully stocked bar and two bed rooms, plus the whole suite was soundproof, so you couldn't hear the music from downstairs in the club.

"These hoes came out tonight, didn't they?" Kirk asked Shane while grabbing a bottle of champagne from the bar.

"Shit! When don't they come out when we ask them to!" Shane responded with his hands in his pockets, standing on the glass floor and looking down into the club.

"The money has been at the drop for four days, and he still hasn't grabbed it yet!" Shane said.

"11 million just sitting in a parked car for four days," Kirk said, then popped the cork on the champagne bottle and took a sip.

"He gon' grab it! He is probably just taking his time, you know. I know he has eyes on it, so nothing's gonna' happen to it!" Kirk added.

"I ain't worried about that, Kirk. I know he is not gonna let anything happen to the money. I think he is about to cut us off!" Shane said.

"Why do you say that?" Kirk asked, sipping from the bottle.

Shane shrugged, then responded, "You know Shorty got locked up!"

Kirk passed back and forth, not really concerned about getting cut off by their supplier or one of their dealers getting locked up. He was protected by the feds.

"That glass floor makes it feel like you're floating when you stand on it, right?" Kirk said, trying to change the subject.

"That's why it's called the sky lounge!" Shane answered sarcastically, then said, "$120,000 and 6 Bricks. Why the fuck was he riding around with all that?"

"Who knows?" Kirk said.

"You think the state troopers turned it over to the feds?" Shane asked.

Kirk shrugs his shoulders, not trying to entertain the conversation. He knows the feds picked the case up already.

"They had to!" Shane continued answering his own question, then moved to another spot on the glass floor to get a better look at something that caught his eye on the dance floor.

"You think that's why Maria didn't pick up the money yet?" Shane asked.

Kirk thinks for a second, trying to choose his words wisely. "Honestly, yea. He probably thinks the feds are watching us like I've been saying!" he answered.

"What the fuck do you mean like you been saying!" Shane snaps, storming off the glass floor towards Kirk. " You know something I don't know?" he yelled.

"Wow, wow!" Kirk said, holding his hands up to stop Shane from getting in his face. "What are you trying to say?" Kirk asked defensively.

Shane stops a few feet in front of Kirk and stares into his eyes, trying to read him. He was having a funny feeling about Kirk, and something wasn't sitting right with him.

"Do you know something I need to know? Let me put it that way?" Shane asked.

Kirk got nervous. He knew the look Shane was giving him. He did know something that Shane needed to know, but it was too late now. Shane was on his own in Kirk's eyes.

"How long have we known each other?" Kirk asked, turning his head away from Shane's glare.

That wasn't an answer to Shane, but he decided to let it go at the moment.

"It's cool. We got 11 million dollars sitting on a street corner for four days. Let's just figure this out first, then deal with everything else. We can't lose that kind of money!" Shane said, walking away from Kirk.

"I think we should let it sit for a couple more days. Give him some time to get to it," Kirk said calmly. Relieved that the attention is off of him.

"We gotta find another connection. All the money we put in this club and the events we got planned. A drought will hurt us right now!" Shane said.

"I'm on it," Kirk said, thinking of how devastated Shane would be when he found out he was the informant.

"Yo! you know that girl right there?" Shane asked, pointing to the red bone he saw earlier, wearing next to nothing. The rainbows coming off the diamonds in her jewelry were blinding from Shane's vantage point.

Kirk walked over to the glass floor and looked. "So that's who you've been over here eye hustling this whole time. No, I don't know her, but she looks good, though."

"I want her tonight!" Shane said, walking off the glass floor to the bar.

"We gon' give three more days to pick the money. If they don't get by, then we go link with the Mexican in Arizona! Fuck it. Unless you find somebody else by then!" Shane said. He grabbed a bottle of D'usse from the bar, opened it, and took a deep gulp. He closed his eyes and gritted his teeth to deal with the burn.

"All those women came out to see us. Come on, let's go have our pick from the litter!" Kirk said, trying to cut through the tension in the air.

"Yeah, how about that? Can't disappoint all the bad bitches. I'm trying to fuck and get my dick sucked on the glass floor. I gotta live up to my reputation." Shane said with a devilish smirk on his face.

Shane and Kirk didn't disappoint. Their special invited guest was a few of their celebrity friends who came through to show their support.

They mingled and partied with everybody until the wee hours of the morning. Shane and the red bone with all the diamonds christened the glass floor.

The red carpet was rolled back out for the exit, and gift bags were handed out to all those who accepted. A bottle of Ace of Spade, a $100 gift card, and a box of condoms.

When the valets started pulling vehicles up, it turned into a car show, Bentleys, BMWs, Benzes,

Audis, Phantoms, Mazaratis; you name it. Music was playing, lights were flashing, and people were taking pictures and going live on social media.

Unbeknown to everybody except for a selected few were the three undercover F.B.I. agents in attendance, checking out the two golden boys and their lavish party.

CHAPTER 8

"You ain't cook yet, Mama?" Chance asked his godmother after walking into the kitchen from the basement. He stretched and then yawned before opening up the refrigerator.

"You got a plate in the microwave!" she said from the living room, sitting in her favorite leather chair by the window where she likes to look outside.

Over the years, she witnessed countless murders through that window. She could look at the side walk on the street and find dark spots that, to the naked eye, looked like blemishes but were really old blood stains. So embedded in the concrete that they become permanent fixtures in the landscape. In some spots, stains over lapped stains. Visual reminders of where the bodies lay until they bled out or were saved.

She witnessed countless drug deals, robberies, shootings, and brutal beatings. Most were committed by kids she knew or knew of.

They say the eyes are the window to a soul, and she considered this window the eyes to hers. She watched the lives that young black kids were burdened with unfold in this neighborhood. The opportunities get snatched away. She watched the most innocent and naive kids turn into the most cold-blooded and violent of them all.

It hurt her heart, and as bad as she wanted to close the blinds on that window and block out the visions her eyes saw, she couldn't. It was her life as well, and she felt like the gatekeeper.

"Damn, what time is it? How long did I sleep?" Chance asked while going to the microwave.

"It's 12:00 a.m.," Mama answered.

"Shit, I've been sleeping for 11 hours! Why didn't you wake me up?" he asked while sitting down at the dining room table with his plate of food.

"I thought about waking you up, but I know how you need your sleep, So I figured I let you rest!" Mama answered.

"Is this all the food left? I know I got more than one plate?" Chance asked.

"I fed Tanisha and Rachel's kids tonight, and I filled my bag up with some plates and took 'em around the corner. Your brother didn't eat his plate!" she said,

Chance looked up at her from the table and asked, "Why?"

"I caught him in the bathroom skitzing and talking to himself again, I don't know what that boy is getting high off of, but he needs to stop!" she said,

"Where did he go?" Chance asked.

"I don't know. He just got mad and left," she answered.

"He took the car?" Chance asked, getting up from the table.

"No, the keys are right here!" Mama held them up.

Chance went into the basement, and a few minutes later, he came back up, putting on his leather jacket. Mama handed him the car keys.

"I'll be back!" Chance said while grabbing them.

"Bring your brother back home and be careful. I'ma be sitting right here until ya'll come home!" Mama added while Chance walked out the door.

He got in the car and called Hammer's cell phone, but it went straight to voicemail. He drove through the strip where they hustled and saw all their Youngbulls standing at the bottom of the block, huddled in a group.

Chance pulled up, rolled the window down, and asked, "What ya'll niggas doing? Why ya'll not up there hustling?"

"Ya brother up there tripping, he shot Antman!" one of them said.

Chance sped up the block and saw Hammer sitting on the front steps of an abandoned house next to the alleyway. At the mouth of the alleyway, he saw a body lying on the ground in a pool of blood. He parked the car and hopped out.

"What the fuck is you doing, brother?" Chance asked while walking up to him.

Hammer had his head down but looked up when he heard Chance's voice.

"Chance, where you been?" he asked.

Chance looked into his eyes and knew that Hammer wasn't himself. He was going through another episode.

Hammer's episodes started when he was a kid, and Chance was the only person who knew about them. Then Mama Meechie came into their lives and eventually found out about them, but she never knew the true extent of them.

The reason behind them was unknown because Hammer never went to a hospital and got his brain examined, talked to a professional about them, or was put on medication. Obviously, he had an underlined mental condition, and mental conditions weren't treated in urban communities. The person was just labeled as being crazy, a rider, or a shot-out.

Hammer's episodes progressively got worse. First, he would beat and torture their pets. Then he started to kill them. When Chance decided to stop taking dogs in, Hammer would kill the neighbors or stray dogs and cats. He outgrew that phase of the episodes once they got into the drug game and began to run the streets. That was when Hammer began to kill people, particularly the customers they became fond of or began to build some kind of relationship with. As they progressed in the drug game and no longer sold it themselves but hired Youngbulls to, Hammer began to kill them. Antman was the second Youngbull he killed.

The episodes weren't as frequent as they were when he was younger, and over the last four years, they came down to three or four a year, but they were more vicious and reckless. Nobody knew what triggered them, but whenever he was caught talking to himself, an episode was sure to follow. It was like he became a different person, real emotional, couldn't sit still, and if he did, his hands or his feet would be moving nonstop.

His eyes, his eyes changed the most. They would get black and glossy and wouldn't focus on anything. He frantically looked and scanned all over the place like he was extremely paranoid or was watching something only he could see that never stopped moving.

If chance wasn't around, Hammer could be stuck in one of his episodes for hours until he eventually pulled himself out, But chance could get him back almost immediately.

After the episode was over, Hammer would go into a deep depression for a day or two, only out of shame and embarrassment, but soon it would get buried somewhere deep in his mind, and he would forget all about it. Chance would too. Hammer was his brother, and their love and bond for each other couldn't be matched by anything or anyone. All they had was each other.

Chance walked over to the body and saw Antman lying there with a chunk of his head missing.

"You killed Antman, brother!" Chance said while Hammer walked over to him.

"My fault, Chance, but that nigga didn't listen," Hammer said.

"What do you mean, that was my Youngbull!" Chance yelled, looking around, trying to assess the situation.

This was their block and neighborhood, and they ruled it with an iron fist. So nobody was calling the police.

"Fuck that nigga Chance. We didn't need him!" Hammer said.

"I told you to stop doing this shit on the block. We can't have homicide around here asking questions and shit, making it hot!" Chance yelled.

"I'm sorry, Chance. You forgive me, right? You forgive me?" Hammer pleaded, grabbing and hugging Chance. "I'm sorry, Chance. You forgive me, right? Don't be mad at me, Chance. You are the only person I got!" Hammer pleaded.

Chance tried to push Hammer off of him, but Hammer was stronger than the average person and kept him in a bear hug.

"Get off me, brother. I ain't mad at you. Let me go!" Chance said nicely and calmly in his brother's ear.

Hammer let Chance go and asked, "You mad at me?"

"Naw, I ain't mad at you, but I need you to snap out of this shit and come back!" Chance said.

"Alright, my brother is not mad at me! My brother is not mad at me!" Hammer said.

Chance grabbed Hammer's face and looked into his eyes. Hammer's eyes were looking everywhere frantically.

"Look at me, brother!" Chance said. "Look at me, brother. Look in my eyes."

Hammer's eyes started to focus on Chance's eyes.

"Right, look me in my eyes, brother. It's me and you, you all I got, brother. You are my only family, and I need you. I need you back so we can deal with this shit out here because I can't do it without you!" Chance said.

"I'm here, Chance!" Hammer said as tears rolled down his cheeks. He always cried during and after an episode.

"You here with me!" Chance asked, wiping the tears off Hammer's cheeks.

"I'm here!" Hammer assured him.

Chance hugged him and said, "I love you, you my brother, and I ain't gon let nothing happen to you or get in between us. It's me and you!"

Chance lets him go and looks into his eyes.

"I love you too, brother," Hammer said, wiping his tears away.

"Ok, we gotta get this body off the block," Chance said.

"I'm ready!" Hammer told him.

"Grab him and pull him in the alleyway. We have to wrap him up in something, throw him in the trunk and drop him off somewhere. We can get one of the Youngbulls to clean the blood up!" Chance said.

Hamer dragged Antman deeper into the alleyway as Chance told him to, then Chance sent one of the Young bulls to buy some trash bags and tape.

Chance went into Antman's pockets and took the little bit of cash he had a cell phone and checked to see if he had any kind of I.D. on him, but he didn't.

Once the trash bags and tape came, Chance and Hammer wrapped Antman's body up as best they could. Chance pulled the car up to the alley, and they put the body in the trunk.

Chance told the Youngbulls to get some soapy water and some bleach and clean the blood up. He told them not to say nothing about what happened to nobody and to not talk about it no more amongst themselves. If anybody asked for Antman, they hadn't seen him and didn't remember the last time they did.

Chance and Hammer drove to a vacant lot that was full of all kinds of trash and debris and dumped Antman's body in the mix. There weren't any houses close by, and lots in Philadelphia usually were vacant for decades before the city sent somebody to clean them out. So by the time, Antman's body was found, it would be just bones, plastic, and a few pieces of raggedy clothes.

"You cool, brother?" Chance asked Hammer, now driving back to the block.

"Yea, I'm alright!" Hammer answered, lifting his head up from staring at his lap.

"You owe me an outfit. You know that, right?" Chance said.

Hammer looked at him and smiled, then put his head back down.

"I need a new pair of Buttas because these got scuffed up. I need a new pair of D. Symone jeans. I need a new B.B.C. hoodie, and you can just put my leather jacket in the cleaners!" Chance said, looking at him.

"It sound like you need a lot nigga!" Hammer responded, lifting his head up and leaning his seat back, trying to get comfortable.

"Yo, brother! What did you tell me about the passenger job?" Chance said.

"Fuck outa here!" Hammer told him.

"Damn, I can't get a new outfit. I could at least get something to smoke?" Chance asked.

Hammer laughed, then went into the glove box and pulled some weed out.

"And don't roll no fucked up L, you hear me, brother!" Chance said jokingly, tapping Hammer's arm.

"Fuck outa here nigga!" Hammer said back, throwing a lil' body shot at Chance's ribs.

"Yo! Mama made fried fish, mac and cheese, spinach, and garlic bread. That shit was poppin', brother. You lucky I ain't eat ya plate!" Chance told him.

"You know better than to eat my food. You remember what happened last time?" Hammer said.

The tension was coming out of his body now. He was feeling more relaxed.

"You can't beat me no more, brother. This ain't the 90s!" Chance said, turning toward him.

Hammer lit the weed and inhaled deeply. He turned to Chance while holding the smoke in his lungs and said, "We need to get some more of this straight up!"

"Hell yea!" Chance responded with a smile, happy that his brother was all the way back with him now, and by the time they finished smoking and joking, everything prior would be a distant memory.

CHAPTER 9

"Maria Munoz!" Detective Alfonso said into the phone, "got it." Date of Birth, August 25, 1958. 1500 Walnut Street, Ashland, PA 17921. All right, I got it. Thanks again, Teressa, no problem!"

Alfonso hung up the phone after getting his friend from the D.M.V. to pull up the owner's information on the forest green Suburban.

He leaned back on his living room couch, it was one of his off days, and he figured he did some investigating himself since Frank was trying so hard to railroad his involvement.

He looked at the name again and knew he was right all along about Frank. Maria Munoz sure didn't seem like a person that was pushing meth for a pagan motorcycle club. Alfonso couldn't help but chuckle to himself and think that he could come up with a better lie than Frank did, or maybe Frank just thought that less of him and figured he would believe anything.

"Ha!" he said out loud to himself. Frank had another thing coming.

The next thing was to find out all the information he could about Maria Munoz because if Frank was interested enough to GPS her car and came up with that weird story, she had to be important or a key piece in whatever Frank was up to.

Alfonso grabbed his laptop computer and went on the narcotic division's web page. He typed in his password and gained access to the database. Then he typed in Maria Munoz's name, date of birth, and her driver's license I.D number, then hit the search button.

While the computer did what it was told, he went into the kitchen for another cup of coffee and a cigarette. He tried to calm his nerves from all the anticipation of what he was about to find out.

* * *

Frank sat on his favorite recliner in front of his big screen t.v and, from his phone, watched the red dot of the GPS tracking device move across the grid of Philadelphia. It was an application that the police force offered, allowing the detectives to monitor the GPS devices from their smartphones or tablets.

He cracked open his 8th can of beer and lit his 6th cigarette. The lil' red dot has been on the move all day. Whoever was driving the forest-green Suburban just seemed to be cruising all over the city, going nowhere in particular.

Frank wondered what it was all about, but it didn't really matter because he knew they had to stop somewhere, and it wasn't going to be back in South Philly. He was patient. He had nothing else to do besides go to Mickey's and drink some more, maybe shoot a couple of games of pool.

He clicked his remote and flipped through the stations on the t.v, but nothing caught his attention. He wasn't a big t.v person anyway. Usually, when he watched it, he ended up daydreaming and missed the whole show. He guzzled his can of beer and took a long pull on the cigarette, his lungs greedy for the carbon-rich smoke.

He wondered what he would do with Alfonso. The kid was cramping his style. Every time he heard his voice, he could feel his blood start to boil in his veins. He knew he couldn't lie to the son of bitch for so long. It would only be a matter of time before he smartened up. Hopefully, he proved himself to be trustworthy so Frank could use him to do all the tedious leg work that he was getting too fat and lazy to do. Fuck it, that was a bridge he would cross when he got to it. For now, the less he knew, the better.

All of a sudden, the lil' red dot stopped moving. Frank enlarged the screen and saw it wasn't at a red light or an intersection, another fast-food restaurant or gas station. It was in the middle of the 1600 block of Franklin St, a few blocks away from Drexel College.

Frank knew that block, but for the love of God, he couldn't remember who he knew about it.

He thought about it some more while he cracked open his 9th can of beer and lit his 7th cigarette, but nothing clicked in his head. It would come to him. Eventually, he thought. It was always like that when he needed to remember something. It didn't pop into his mind until he wasn't thinking about it anymore. It mostly happens with names, birthdays, or any kind of date.

He looked at the red dot, and it was still there. If it stayed in one spot longer than a half hour, the next time it moved, it would send Frank an alert. Might as well get dressed, he figured, swing past Franklin St, and sit around for a few minutes to see if he can see something or someone. After that, he could go to Mickey's and monitor the movements from there. It was slow but progressed nonetheless.

* * *

After his coffee and cigarette, Alfonso went back to his laptop and saw that the search was complete. He grabbed his notebook and pen, then sat down to write what he found.

Maria Munoz and her mother, Gloria Munoz, immigrated to the United States from Nicaragua in 1983. Her father, Carmelo Munoz, was a high-ranking member of the rebel national army and died in the civil war in 1981. Her only brother Carmelo Munoz jr' who was also a high-ranking member of the rebel national army, Immigrated to the United States in 1982.

Alfonso remembered a lil' bit about the civil war in Nicaragua from history class, and he also read about some of the conspiracies behind the war.

The United States allied with Nicaragua's President and supposedly had a great interest in the developing country, which Nicaragua's President wasn't trying to adhere to. Allegedly, the United States government sent the C.I.A. to Nicaragua to train and rouse up The Rebel National Army so they could overthrow their current president and government. Basically, giving the United States control of the country by having control of the rebels. The C.I.A. also allegedly let some Nicaraguan immigrants into the United States smuggle narcotics and use the money to help fund the war in what became known as the Nicaraguan Contra.

Some of the immigrants went back to help fight the war, but most stayed in the United States and took advantage of the opportunity that the government gave them to flourish in the drug game at the beginning of its height. The real Rick Ross from California said that it was a Nicaraguan immigrant that supplied him with his cocaine, and countless others also made that claim.

Alfonso also read that Maria Munoz lived in San Francisco, California, from 1983 to 1990 and, in those seven years, was arrested twice for possession of a controlled substance. Both cases were taken to trial, and both cases were dismissed.

Her mother, Gloria Munoz, died of heart complications in 1988. In 1990 Maria moved to Arizona. In 1992 she moved to Atlanta, and in 1994 she moved to Pennsylvania and had basically never been in trouble or heard from since. No traffic violations or any kind of citations. She had no kids and was never married.

Her brother Carmelo Munoz jr' paper trail stopped once he entered the United States. No I.D., no job, never had anything in his name. He basically fell off the face of the earth. Maria had no other known relatives in the country.

Alfonso wondered if Maria was a result of the Nicaraguan contra because she immigrated during the time and had two drug arrests. He also wondered what had happened to her brother and how he could just disappear like that. His biggest question was what the hell Frank was trying to track her for, and could she possibly still be in the drug game? He doubted it, but he had to find out because Frank wouldn't be going through all this for no reason. Then he figured if it was true, he could bust Maria and frank. Just these two cases would be career-making cases. He had to keep pursuing them.

If it took for him to be lied to, and to be Frank's flunky just so he could get information and do his own investigation, then that's what it was going to be. If he gained Frank's trust and Frank opened up to him, that would be even better. Every man had his price, and Alfonso just found his.

* * *

Frank lounged around his house for another hour and a half, drinking the rest of his beers and smoking cigars, only getting up to go to the bathroom and piss when he told himself he was gonna get dressed and leave.

He finally climbed out of his recliner, stretched, and yawned. He looked down at his old raggedy old recliner and smiled in admiration of it. It took years for a man to break into his favorite chair. It took time for the chair to form to the contours of his body and adjust to the way he leaned and slouched when he sat in it.

Frank loved that chair, and if you asked his second wife, he loved it more than he loved her. To anybody else, the chair looked like it was one sitting away from crumpling to the floor into a pile of twisted springs, broken wood, and worn-out leather. To Frank, it looked like a cloud that God sent from heaven for him to rest upon.

He looked around his living room at all the empty beer cans and the ashtray full of cigarette buts. The empty potato chip bags and the plates of half-eaten sandwiches and pie crust. He knew he had to clean up. If his daughter was to stop and pass to see the place looking like this, she would tear him a new asshole. She could be so cruel and vicious with her words. She knew exactly what to say to cut a man deep and wondered why she wasn't married with children yet.

He cleaned up, then dragged himself up the steps into the bathroom to shit, shower, and shave, which took him another two hours before he was finally dressed and heading out the door.

While walking to his car, he got an alert on his phone informing him that the red dot was on the move from Franklin St. He sat in his car, pulled the application up, and watched the red dot start to cruise around again. He thought about trailing the Suburban for a while, but it was too early for that much pressure, and he didn't want to risk exposing himself before he was in a position to come for what he wanted. Plus, that was what the GPS. was for. So he could do his police work with comfort and convenience until it was time to strike, so he decided to head to Mickey's. All those cans of beer just made his throat dry, so it was time for some hard liquor to quench his thirst.

Frank sat at the bar in Mickey's and drank with his few buddies and talked shit as they usually do. It wasn't a day that went past that Frank didn't visit Mickey's. He liked the crowd of people who came in every day to drink and talk. He liked the smell, the colors, and the old upholstery. Just the whole atmosphere was appealing to him. He was as comfortable in there as he was sitting in his chair.

He watched the red dot continue to cruise around the city, stop at another fast food restaurant and then stop on 5th and South Street at a bar Frank knew called 'The wild goose.' That was one thing he had no problem remembering, the names and locations of bars. He wondered what the business was behind that stop. The wild goose wasn't a place for somebody like Maria. It was mostly white rowdy college kids in there.

After a few hours, a full bottle of Jack Daniel, and a couple of games of darts, he sat there and watched the red dot go on the move again.

He started to recognize a familiar route it was driving. It was the route Frank took when he drove home. That began to alarm him, but he brushed it off as just a coincidence. There was no reason for the Suburban to be heading in that direction, and he was sure it was gonna turn off at some point.

Then it pulled up on his block and stopped in front of his house. Frank's heart almost jumped out of his chest. He snatched his phone, ran out of the bar, got in his car, and raced toward his home.

It couldn't be, he thought.

Did Maria find out about him and send some of her goons in the Suburban to his house to kill him? She couldn't be that stupid because if she found out about him, then she would know his reputation and how he lived up to it.

Then again, he wasn't even sure if Maria was into what he expected her to be, but it had to be true because why the fuck was the Suburban doing at his house.

He ran through stop sign after stop sign, red light after red light. It was the luck of the Irish that he didn't cause a traffic accident and draw the attention of the State Troopers.

Frank had his snub nose 357 revolver in his shoulder holster, but that was his bar gun, small up close and personal. He couldn't get in a shootout with that. He reached into his glove box and pulled out his 45-caliber handgun and sat it in his lap. *This would work*, he thought.

He pulled up to his block doing 60 miles an hour and came to a screeching halt in front of his house. He jumped out of the car, gun in hand, and was surprised when he didn't see the Suburban. He looked up and down the block and still didn't see it. He looked at his phone, and the GPS showed it was still in front of his house. *It's gotta be some kind of mistake*, he thought.

It was a Global Positioning Satellite. How could it make a mistake like this?

Frank left his car in the middle of the street in the park with the engine running and the driver's side door open. He walked on the sidewalk in front of his house and wondered what the heck was going on.

All of a sudden, his front door opened, and his daughter's head popped out. "Dad! What's going on?" she asked.

Looking concerned as to why he would pull up in front of the house like that in the middle of the night and then be standing on the sidewalk pissy drunk with his gun in his hand, looking crazy.

"Martha!" Frank yelled, turning to look at her. "What the fuck are you doing here?" he demanded.

"Excuse me!" his daughter said, shocked by the way he spoke to her. "I was at The Wild Goose. I didn't feel like driving all the way home, so I came here! Why? What's going on, and why do you have your gun in your hand? Jesus, Frank, are you drunk?" she said.

"The Wild Goose!" Frank said to himself. It didn't make sense. He looked back at his phone, and the red dot was still in front of his house.

"You were on Franklin Street today?" he asked her.

"Yes, Dad. Now, if you could please tell me what's going on because if you are in one of ya drunk, crazed illusions, I could just go back to my friend's house!" she answered.

Frank put his gun on his hip, then finally noticed his daughter's car parked in front of his house. He had an idea. He had a portable bug detector device in the trunk of his car. He retrieved it and scanned over his daughter's car and found a GPS device under the left rear wheel well.

"It can't be," he said to himself.

On a little piece of paper in his wallet, he had the serial number written down to the GPS Alfonso placed on the Suburban.

He pulled his wallet out, found it, and compared it to the serial number on the one he just took off his daughter's car. It was a match.

"Son of a bitch!" he mumbled as the realization of what happened started to settle in his mind and sent a cold chill up his spine.

An eerie feeling of him being watched started to play on his paranoia. His safety was compromised; to make matters worse, this was an indirect threat to his daughter's life. Letting Frank know that he could be touched as well.

He drove to south Philly just to see if the Suburban was gone, and it was.

CHAPTER 10

"I'm out front!" Shane said on his cell phone, then hung up.

He was sitting in his all-black TrackHawk, parked in front of one of Kirk's houses in Reading, Pennsylvania.

A few minutes later, Kirk came out and got into the passenger seat of the car. "It's 5 am. This could have waited until the sun came up!" he said while rubbing one of his eyes with his hand.

"Money, don't sleep, playa!" Shane responded while leaning back in his seat, texting on his phone.

"It's too early for this shit, man. What's up?" Kirk asked, annoyed and not feeling like playing.

Kirk took a deep breath and let the air out slowly through his nostrils. Shane was unpredictable sometimes, and with Kirk snitching, he was becoming more and more paranoid about him finding out.

"What's up, man? Do you have an address or something? Maria hit you up?" Kirk asked, looking at Shane.

Shane put his phone in his pocket and said, "You already know we're back on deck!" Not able to hide the excitement in his voice.

"When did they pick up the car and the money?" Kirk asked, a little skeptical.

"I don't know! I just got a text with an address. I didn't text or call back. You already know what it is! You might as well go get dressed so we can handle this business," Shane told him.

Kirk felt that Shane's mood was off, but he wasn't going to be getting spoken to like that by anyone.

"Why are you talking to me like that?" Kirk asked him.

"Talking to you like what?" Shane said, looking over at him.

They stared at each other for a second. Kirk could feel the tension coming from Shane. *Was this the back, was he gone cross me and take all the work for himself*? Kirk thought.

Then Shane smiled at him and said, "How long have we known each other, Kirk?"

The hairs on Kirk's arms rose. *This is it. I'm done with Shane after this.*

His conscience was eating him up, and he couldn't trust Shane anymore. He was gonna disappear and let the feds handle what they needed to. Then come back in a few years and pick up the pieces without Shane.

"Long enough!" Kirk answered.

"Let's get this show on the road then. We have a lot to do!" Shane said.

"Cool!" Kirk replied, hopping out of the car to get dressed and ready.

Shane pulled his phone out and finished texting.

A few minutes later, Kirk came back out dressed and carrying a Gucci book bag. He opened the passenger door, threw the bag in the backseat, and asked, "Where are we picking them up from? What's the address?"

Shane started the car and pulled off before answering him. "2020 Parnell Lane, Upper Darby, Pennsylvania!" Shane answered.

"Those houses have garages in the back, right?" Kirk asked.

"Yeah!" Shane answered.

Kirk wondered if the feds were following them now, and if Shane was to back door him, would they swoop in to help? His thoughts were all over the place. He was stressed out. He couldn't eat, and he couldn't sleep. He was losing it. He just wanted it all to be over.

"We compress them from 300 bricks to 450. We compress the 100 bricks of Fetty to 250, right?" Kirk asked, trying to get his head back in the game.

"Absolutely, we gotta make this one count, playa!" Shane answered nonchalantly.

Kirk never carried a gun, but lately, he has. He reached into the back seat and grabbed his book bag where he had it, and put the bag on his lap.

"We are taking them to the Hit Factory in West Philly, right? Because that's the only place big enough to cover our order A.S.A.P!" Kirk said, hoping Shane would go with the play.

The feds have been watching the Hit Factory for decades, and Kirk knew it wouldn't be long before they raided. He felt safe any place he knew they were investigating.

"That will work!" Shane said, still texting while he was driving.

Jonah Brown owned the Hit Factory. He was known in the drug game as a Master Chef. Cooking, cutting, and compressing cocaine, heroin, or fentanyl was just as important in the drug game as selling it.

A Master Chef could tell you what region of the world the cocaine came from. The method that was used when it was cultivated and what it was cut with or if it was cut at all.

They could strip a bad cut from a product without losing its potency, then re-cut it with something to make it jump from a five into a seven or an eight on the scale of potency.

Most drug dealers couldn't master that art. If they did, they didn't have time to be in the kitchen manufacturing. They were in the trap. Most major drug dealers paid a Master Chef to cook, cut and manufactured the raw product to meet their customers' demands.

Jonah Brown got business because he was honest and trustworthy. He never stole a gram and made a name for himself during the crack epidemic of the 80s and 90s. Over the years, his reputation grew among the elite in the drug game. Therefore, his clientele grew. He never aspired to be a drug dealer. He was content with the lane he made for himself.

With all the demands, he had to expand, so he bought an old Tastykake warehouse and named it The Hit Factory. His new kitchen and place of business, and he only took orders of 100 bricks of cocaine or better.

The hit factory had top-of-the-line security cameras on the corners of every block within a 30-block radius to monitor the movements of the police and to watch all the parking lots and ducky blocks in the area where the cops gathered before making a raid.

In addition to the police scanners, all the doors from the Hit Factory were reinforced with U.S grade A steel and would damn near take a tank to get through. In the decade and a half that the hit factory has been operating, it has never been raided by the police and never been robbed, but Kirk knew records were meant to be broken.

"They got everything we need. All we have to do is place the order and drop the work off. They will let us know when to come get it!" Kirk told him.

"How much that's gon' run us?" Shane asked.

"I say around $250,000 all together!" answered Kirk.

"And all we gotta do is drop it off and pick it up?" Shane asked.

"We can stay there with it if we want, but I'm cool!" Kirk told him, knowing it could get raided at any moment.

"Whatever you want to do as far as that. Imma let you run the play, so everything goes smooth," Shane said.

Kirk thought, *Ok, so if anything goes wrong, it's my fault. He wants to leave the responsibility on me to secure the flip. That's cool.*

"I'ma get in touch with Johna and let him know we're gonna be there today!" Kirk told him.

"Cool!" Shane said.

Shane and Kirk rode in silence for the rest of the way to Upper Darby. Both of them were in deep contemplation. Texting and calling their few customers to let them know that they were back on deck and to place their orders while they could.

The drug game was like wall street. Coke prices were up and down. Buy your drugs while they are cheap because the more who buy, the fewer shares left. That will drive the price of the rest of the product significantly.

So, you could get a brick of cocaine for $17,500 right now, depending on how many you get. At the end of the month, that same brick might cost between $28,000 to $32,000.

When Shane and Kirk got to the address of the drop, they went into the basement and found all the bricks stacked in a corner on skids. This wasn't the first time getting this large amount of drugs, but no matter how many times they scored, when they walked into a room and saw all that work, it gave them an overwhelming feeling of accomplishment.

It was unexplainable. Even if the feds raided right then and there, just being able to have felt that feeling alone would give them gratification until the end of their bid. It was the feeling that few men in the drug game got to feel, and many died trying to feel. Now the task was getting it to the Hit Factory.

Chapter 11

"Jump in, younging!" Chance said to one of his dealers, named 'Problem,' out of the driver's side window after pulling up on him.

Problem looks up and down the block nervously before getting in, a gesture that didn't go unnoticed by Chance.

"What's up with you, Bull? Why you looking around like you just saw a ghost or something?" Chance asked while pulling off.

"Naw, it ain't nothing, Oldhead!" Problem said, not able to hide the fear in his voice.

Chance stopped at the top of the block where Hammer was talking to a couple of the other Youngbulls. Hammer walked over to the passenger side window and leaned in.

"Where you going?" Hammer asked.

"I'm about to make a run real quick. I'll be back in like 5 minutes!" Chance answered.

"Grab me a bottle of E&J from the liquor store," Hammer asked.

"E&J!" Chance said, frowning. "Come on with that old man shit, brother. You want a bottle of Casamigos or something?" Chance asked.

"If I wanted a bottle of Casamigos, I would've said that. I want some E&J!" Hammer told him.

Hammer then tapped Problem on his shoulder and said, "What's up, younging? Why do you have your head down like that? What are you sad about?"

Problem gave hammer a weak grin while lifting his head and trying not to make eye contact with him.

"What's wrong with this nigga?" Hammer asked Chance while pointing at Problem.

"He's cool?" Chance assured him. "E&J, I'll be back in 5 minutes!" he finished.

"Ard!" Hammer said, then walked away from the car and back to the conversation he was having with the Youngbulls.

Chance pulled off and headed to the liquor store.

"Look, you're about to casework the block now!" Chance told Problem.

Problem looked out the passenger side window for a long second, then said, "I mean, if you need me to fuck it, I'll do it!"

"You sound like you not happy! What's up? All you gotta do is drop off the work, pick up the money and make sure they are out there hustling when they are supposed to be. Unless you want to hug the block and hand to hand all ya life!" Chance said.

He was feeling a weird vibe from Problem since the situation with Antman. He wanted to get him alone, pick his brain and see what was on his mind.

"Honestly, I'd rather hug the block!" Problem said.

"You rather hug the block! For what? You make more money doing case-working!" Chance told him.

Problem didn't say anything.

"You don't hear me talking to you?" Chance asked him.

"Yea, I hear you!" Problem answered.

He definitely has an issue, Chance thought. "Look, younging, we are not gon' beat around the bush. I've been getting a funny feeling from you lately, so whatever you got on ya mind, you better spit it out now!" he told Problem.

Problem thought for a second, trying to choose his words wisely. Then said, "I'm not tryna get on ya brother's bad side, that's all."

Chance was confused. "How do you think being a caseworker will put you on my brother's bad side? What do you mean by that?" Chance asked, looking over at him.

"I mean, look at Booda and Antman! First, Booda starts case-working, and one day Hammer tells him to take a ride with him but never brings Booda back. Then the next day, they find Booda dead on the back street! Now Antman! Antman wasn't doing anything. We were chilling. Hammer comes up and tells Antman to take a walk with him, and then he shoots him in his head in front of the ally," Problem said.

He looked over at Chance to see what he was going to say, but when he kept quiet, Problem continued to talk, "It's like, when people casework the block, they get close to you. You be putting people on game, yameen. How to manage the block? They gotta make runs with you. Going out to party and chill sometimes! Your brother don't like that. When people start getting close to you, he feels some type of way about it! You have to know what I'm talking about, Chance!" Problem pleaded with him.

He waited for a response from Chance, but he didn't say anything. He just leaned his car seat back and drove while he thought about what Problem had just said to him.

The dogs they had when they were younger, Chance thought.

He loved those dogs. When he started spending more time with the dogs than he did with Hammer, that's when Hammer would have an episode and kill the dogs.

Chance pulled in front of the liquor store and parked. "Hold up, younging!" he told Problem, then got out of the car and went into the store while still thinking.

He thought about the few customers that Hammer killed. Some of them Chance called Auntie, Mom, or Unk because they reminded him of those kinds of figures. All of them took a liking to Chance and favored him over the other hustlas. One by one, Hammer eventually killed them all.

Chance got the liquor, then got back in the car and pulled off.

"Ima take you with me to grab this work real quick!" he told Problem.

"Ard… we cool, right?" Problem asked, not knowing how to take Chance.

"Yea, we're straight young!" Chance said, grinning at him, then falling back into deep thought.

Chance knew Problem was right about Booda and Antman. Hammer was his brother, though, and Chance was his brother's keeper — what he was supposed to do. He and his brother protected each other at all costs. They knew no other way.

Chance made a quick detour and drove to 43rd and Hutton Street in West Philadelphia. Hutton Street was called death row because there were only three houses that were lived in, and those three were homes of drug addicts. The rest of the block was filled with vacant lots and abandoned houses.

Chance pulled into the middle of the block and parked.

"What are we doing here?" Problem asked.

"I gotta grab something real quick, come on!" he said to Problem while getting out of the car.

Problem hopped out and followed chance into one of the abandoned houses.

"What do we have to get from out of here?" Problem asked, looking around suspiciously. He had a funny feeling about Chance all of a sudden.

"It's a bag of 8 Balls I need from here!" Chance said while leading him into the kitchen.

Problem went in his pants pocket and turned his cell phone on, then put it in his hoodie pocket. Behind Chance's back, he opened the Instagram app and went live while the phone was still in his pocket. Only the audio was being recorded.

He knew something wasn't right and was praying somebody would join his live feed in case something happened to him. He now regretted saying anything to Chance about his brother.

"You see that hole over there in the corner?" Chance asked while pointing to a corner in the kitchen.

"Yea, I see it!" Problem answered, looking in the direction Chance was pointing.

"It's a bag of 8 Balls in there. Stick ya hand in that jawn and grab it for me!" Chance told him.

Problem looked at Chance and began to panic. He looked around the room for a way to run out, but Chance was blocking the door. For a brief second, he thought about rushing past him and trying to make it out, but he knew Chance's finger was on the trigger of his gun, which was now in his jacket pocket.

So he decided to play it cool. *Maybe it is a test*, Problem thought.

"Stick my hand in the hole! It's probably rats and all kinds of stuff in there! I'm not doing that!" Problem said, his voice cracking from fear.

Chance took a step closer to him, Problem took a step back to keep some space between them.

"Stop bitching. You don't trust me or something? What do you think Ima do to you here?" Chance asked.

"Nothing!" Problem said, keeping his cool.

"Well, stick ya hand in there and grab the bag of 8 Balls!" Chance demanded.

Problem took a deep breath to build his confidence, then he kneeled in the corner and stuck his hand in the hole. "I don't feel anything," he said after a second or two.

"It's in there. I checked this morning. Just stick ya hand in further and feel around!" Chance said while walking up behind him.

Problem reached his hand in the hole up to his elbow and began to feel around.

"You feel it now?" Chance asked, standing directly behind Problem, pulling out his Glock 40 Handgun.

"I think I can feel something! It's a plastic bag?" Problem asked.

Chance put the gun to the back of Problem's head and pulled the trigger.

'BOOM!'

The sound from the blast echoed through the abandoned house, scaring the rats and rodents and sending them scurrying about.

Problem's brains splattered over the wall, and his body slumped in the corner headfirst. His hand was still in the rat hole.

"You feel that dick head?" Chance said to his lifeless body before turning and leaving the house.

Chance had to kill Problem. He couldn't let him be around knowing his brother's secret.

* * *

Hammer was still out there talking to the other Youngbulls when Chance pulled back up on the block. He parked the car, grabbed the bottles of liquor, and hopped out.

They all looked over at him and noticed that Problem wasn't with him. No one asked because it was none of their business.

Chance passed Hammer the bottle, and Hammer embraced him in a hug to whisper something in his ear. "You were on death row?" he asked.

"How do you know?" Chance answered.

"Because the leather on ya Gucci sneaks all dusty," Hammer said.

Chance looked down at his shoes and whispered back in Hammer's ear, "Yea, I wasn't feeling him, so I sent him home!"

Hammer pulled back from his embrace while smiling. He then cracked the bottle open and took a long gulp. He passed it to Chance, and he did the same.

If chance killed Problem then Hammer knew he had a good reason. There was no need for him to inquire about it because with killing came a certain level of embarrassment and shame. Homicides were never discussed among killers.

Chance took another sip of the liquor, then passed it back to Hammer and joined in on the frivolous conversation they were having before looking at his watch and noticing the time.

"Oh, shit!" Chance said. We gotta go meet John. I almost forgot!"

Chance passed Hammer the car keys. They shook the Youngbulls' hands and told them to be on point. Then they hopped in the car and left.

They were down to their last couple of ounces of cocaine and had to re-up. They were supposed to meet their connection on 58th and Lansdowne Avenue in West Philadelphia.

"Yo, we on our way!" Chance said into the phone, then hung up as Hammer turned out of their block into traffic.

"Roll up! You know ya job!" Hammer said jokingly, then turned out of traffic and onto the main street. He got caught at a red light at the intersection.

"Fuck off here, brother!" Chance responded, then reached in the glove block to grab the weed and roll up.

All of a sudden, a minivan pulled up on the passenger side of their car. The sliding door opened, revealing a person holding an A.K 47 assault rifle.

Chance saw it out of the corner of his eye. Hammer stepped on the gas and sped away, but he was a second too late. Chance couldn't duck out of the shooter's line of vision.

He opened fire on the car, showering the interior with bullets and broken glass from the window. Hammer raced away up the street, trying to get away from the minivan and the gun fire, but the van didn't give chase. The damage was done.

Chance lay slumped in the passenger seat, blood spilling from his face, back, and chest.

CHAPTER 12

"He's one of yours?" Detective Washington asked Frank after dropping a file on his desk.

Frank picked up the file, opened it, and breezed through it. "No shit! When did this happen?" Frank asked, surprised.

"Yesterday," Washington answered.

"What's going on with his brother?" Frank asked.

"We have been looking for him for the last 24 hours, nobody saw him or heard from him. We have their Godmother, Ms. Douglas, in the interrogation room right now," Washington said.

"Really!" Frank said, pausing for a minute in contemplation. "Do you mind if I listen in?" he then asked.

"That's what I'm here for, buddy, your narcotics were homicide, and since he's on your caseload, it's only right you be a part of it. Plus, I figured, you know, maybe we could collaborate and work on the case together because I'm pretty sure this isn't gonna be the end of it," Washington said.

Frank thought about it for a minute. The two brothers were at the bottom of Frank's investigation and not really that significant. They weren't making enough money to afford Frank's time and attention. They weren't major players. Even though they were associated with a few, they were mostly known for robberies and shooting. He didn't have anything to lose, why not let detective Washington do all the work for him, and all he has to do is what he has been doing. Besides sharing a few notes here and there.

"Sure, why not?" Frank said while straightening his chair. "Well, what happened?" he asked.

"What we know so far is that somebody dropped the kid off at Ms. Douglas' house, all shot up, and then left. She put him in the back seat of her car and drove him to the hospital," Washington said.

"Who dropped him off?" Frank asked.

"She said that she never saw the person before, but we assume it was his brother. We got a few calls about a shooting on 55th and Greenway in Southwest Philly, which is a couple blocks away from Ms. Douglas' house. When the officers arrived at the scene, all they found was broken glass from a car windshield and a few spent shell casings from an A.K 47 assault rifle," Washington said.

"Did Demetrius give a description of the car and the driver that dropped the kid off at her house?" Frank asked.

"Said she was too distraught and didn't pay attention long enough to remember. Her only focus was getting the kid to the hospital. We asked her to look through some photos of his known associates, which really ain't many, but she refused to," Washington said.

"What about ballistics?" Frank asked.

"Three of the bullets went in and out. They pulled a fourth from his body during the surgery but were still waiting for the ballistics to confirm the caliber. Just off eye sight, it looks like the same caliber from the shooting on 55th and Greenway," Washington said.

Frank thought for a few seconds and then asked, "What she's saying about his brother."

"Nothing, she refuses to answer any questions about him," Washington answered.

"She's not gon' cooperate at all," Frank said.

"That's what it's looking like, but we just got her in there as part of the procedure. There's really no reason to keep her any longer. I figure we will question her some more while we can about her involvement with the brothers and all these criminals over the years. Hopefully, we can shake her up a lil' bit and try to catch her in a few lies," Washington said.

"What the doctors said about the kid?" Frank asked.

"He made it through surgery, and he's in a medically induced coma now, on life support. They gave him a 20% chance of survival," Washington answered.

"Jeez!" Frank said, balling up his face. "Let's hope he pulls through because I heard some nasty stuff about his brother. You might want to get a hold of him as soon as possible!" Frank added.

"We're looking. Every squad car is riding around with a picture of him. If the rumors are true, it won't be long before we cross paths with him. I believe this godmother of theirs knows where he is," Washington said.

"Well, let's see what else she has to say," Frank said, standing up from his desk and stretching.

He looked up at Alfonso, who was having a conversation on the phone. Frank figured he should hurry up and leave before he saw him and tried to tag along. He put an extra pep in his step and left the office with detective Washington.

* * *

It was a camera inside the interrogation room that allowed the other detectives the luxury of watching interrogations on a t.v screen from another room. When Frank got to the monitoring room, he took his seat and looked at the screen.

Demetrius was sitting at the square table in the room, nursing a cup of coffee with a blank expression on her face. She would sip the coffee, put the cup down, and lean back in her seat with her hand over her face covering her eyes. She was clearly uncomfortable, agitated, and stressed out.

Frank watched her for a couple of minutes before asking, “Who’s doing the interview?”

“My partner, Williams!” answered Washington. “He ate from taco bell last night, bad burrito or something. Been in and out the bathroom all day. He should be back in a couple of minutes!” Washington said.

Frank frowned, not needing to know that much information about Williams’ bowel movements. Washington must’ve read his expression the wrong way because he added, “Tell me about it! I bet he wiped himself raw by now!”

Frank ignored him, not trying to entertain the conversation. Instead, he put his attention back on Demetrius Douglas. Frank knew his fair share of her, and at one point, she became the focus of one of his investigations.

* * *

A few years back, when Frank was still in homicide, she was involved with a well-known drug dealer named ‘Rasheed Akron’ who Frank was trying to tax. Rasheed was elusive, and Frank couldn’t corner him. He went on a campaign and arrested several of his workers and passed on numerous messages for Rasheed to get with his program, But it wasn’t enough to convince him. He would just bail the workers out of jail, pay for lawyers, and or hire new workers.

It wasn't until a confidential informant told Frank that Demetrius introduced Rasheed to his cocaine supplier, and in return, she was being paid a small percentage of the profits every time Rasheed would re-up. With this information, Frank's focus went from Rasheed to Demetrius. Frank dove into her background and found she had several petty arrests for prostitutions, small possession of controlled substances, public intoxication, loitering, and trespassing. She basically had a record of a drug addict. She was in and out of rehabs, and all kinds of centers for abused and battered women, mostly all were court-ordered.

Then out of nowhere, she voluntarily signed into a long-term program and successfully completed it. A year later, she started a nonprofit organization called 'They Care Demetrius' and has been relatively clean ever since, despite her affiliation with the characters outside her organization and the speculations behind them.

It seemed that every one of the children she became involved with became more involved with the streets, and the rumor was that her nonprofit was the cover for a gang that she was allegedly the head of. That's where the nicknames 'Godmother and Meechie boys' came from. Her top earners were called Meechie boys, a title that the other kids aspired to claim. After more research, Frank found out that she paid bail for her kids, hired lawyers, went to court to support them and spoke on their behalf, put money on their prison accounts, and would frequently visit a few.

Now, if that made her the head of the gang or not, Frank didn't know because, from the outside looking in, that was what it seemed like. Even though it was kind of far-fetched to suggest that a woman could manipulate and control a pack of street kids like that, whatever the case was. Frank became determined to find out.

Unfortunately, Frank's investigation came to an abrupt end when Rasheed was murdered, which led to a drug war between rival dealers over Rasheed's clientele and turf. To make matters worse for Frank, he found out that Rasheed was also being investigated by the feds for a Federal Indictment under the Rico law and the C.C.E as well as Demetrius Douglas for conspiracy to launder money and tampering with evidence in an attempt to hinder a federal investigation.

After Rasheed's death and the bloody drug war that claimed most of the lives of his associates, the F.B.I.'s case went to shit, and charges were never filed against Demetrius, and with the murder rate soaring from the war, Frank lost interest in her as well.

Frank knew that Hammer and Chance were now her Meechie boys and still suspected that she had her hand in their street affairs somehow, But since Rasheed, all of her Meechie boys never made it past low or mid-level dealers. That wasn't worth any of Frank's time or effort it took to tax them. Although Hammer and Chance showed a lil' promise, with Chance on life support now and Hammer somewhere probably roaming around the streets like a mad serial killer out for vengeance, it seemed like she raised another unsuccessful pair of Meechie boys.

"Do you mind if I ask her a few questions?" Frank said.

"Sure, be my guest!" answered Washington.

Frank figured he might as well give a crack at her for entertainment purposes. Get his mind off Maria Munoz for a while, and maybe he would be able to come up with some fresh ideas because, at this point, he was at a stand still. David Cameron, who gave him the lead for Maria and the Suburban, was pissed because he blew it.

David provided the intel, and Frank was the muscle, and David would basically have to jump through hula hoops to get another lead on Maria because the green suburban was never spotted again. No other cars were registered in her name, her last known address was abandoned, and no forwarding address was available.

"Tell Williams to knock on the door when he gets out the John!" Frank said to Washington while getting up and going into the interrogation room.

* * *

After hanging up the phone with his sister, Alfonso sat at his desk and wondered if he should pursue the new tip he got. He wanted to wait for one of his off days so he wouldn't draw attention from Frank, but he knew when information came your way, you had to follow up on it while you could. Plus, he figured Frank wouldn't miss him for a couple of hours and would probably be pleased to see him not in the office and try to sneak out himself.

It wasn't hard for Alfonso to find out that Frank's investigation into Maria wasn't going as he had planned because Alfonso found the GPS that he had put on her car back in its original box in Frank's trunk. How Frank got it back, he didn't know.

The way Frank was looking over his shoulder and flinching at unexpected sounds led Alfonso to believe that Maria or one of her associates found it and gave it back to him personally. Probably with a message attached to it.

Alfonso wanted to question Frank about it but decided not to. Frank would just lie some more. Alfonso found some pleasure in knowing that Maria put fear in Frank's heart, and that distant look he's been having in his eyes lately put a smile on Alfonso's face. Alfonso couldn't help but feel a little guilty at the same time because no matter what, Frank was still a member of the police force, and the safety and well-being of another officer were the priority. But as far as Alfonso was concerned, Frank's safety and well-being weren't a concern, and the distress he felt, he deserved for being an asshole. So this was a guilt Alfonso could live with.

Alfonso had seen Frank slip out of the office with detective Washington and knew that if he was gonna follow up on his new tip, now was the time to do it.

"Fuck it," he said to himself. *To be a good detective, you gotta take initiative.*

So he gathered his things and left the office.

* * *

"How are you doing, Ms. Douglas?" Frank asked after entering the room.

He extended his hand for a friendly shake, but the gesture was ignored by Demetrius. Frank's hand was left extended until he pulled it back awkwardly and had a seat.

"Why am I still here?" Demetrius asked him with her hands clasped together in her lap.

"Well, I have a few more questions to ask, if you don't mind," Frank answered.

"First of all, I do mind because I answered every question I was asked in regard to what happened to my Godson last night. There's no further information I can give about what happened that I didn't already give to detective Williams and Washington. Second of all, you're a narcotic detective! So, what are you even here for?" she said,

Frank was caught off by the tone of her voice. It was sweet and had a slight southern drawl, even though she was born and raised on the east coast. It was the tongue of Philadelphia. It carried an air of dignity, respect, and authority. She spoke with the strength of experience and wisdom that one could only gain from a hard life on the streets.

Frank stuttered, trying to respond, and managed to say, "First of all, I'm here because this is my place of employment. Second of all, your Godson was involved in narcotics, and I'm assuming that this shooting had something to do with it!"

"Well, don't make an ass out of yourself by assuming, Frank! Now, I'ma tell you, just like I told the other two detectives. I have nothing to say about what y'all assume my Godson was involved with!" Demetrius said.

"If I may say so, Ms. Demetrius, I was an ass way before I started assuming, and I'm really a jackass when I'm drunk if you let any of my wives tell it. Now you know just as well as I do that your Godson was in the drug game. I'm just gonna be Frank about it, no pun intended. Maybe you have seen his supplier before, heard a name spoken around you in reference to drugs or something of that nature. Any kind of info would be helpful no matter how minute you may think it is," Frank said.

Without missing a beat, Demetrius said, "Since we're being frank, Frank. I know who you are, what you do, and what you represent. It's no secret, even though you might think it is, but it's not. You're nothing but a crook hiding behind a badge, trying to rob the robbers and hustle the hustlers. If you're interested in any information, then it's for your own personal, greedy, piggish gain!"

Frank's face flushed red with embarrassment as he felt his blood pressure start to rise. *How dare she speak to me like that*! he thought.

He turned his chair so he was directly facing her, and his back was to the camera. He leaned toward her as close as he could so she could hear him talk through his clenched teeth.

"You think you know me, Lady, but you have no idea! I'm more than just a crook, I'm everything above, but you think you have the right to judge me when you're just as bad as me. Hiding beyond your nonprofit and taking them bastard kids off the streets and teaching them how to deal drugs and kill people. I know who you are and all about you too. Think you all high and mighty now because you don't smoke crack no more!" Frank snarled at her.

Frank's words cut her deep. She raised her hand and swung it to slap Frank's face, but he caught her arm by the wrist.

He smiled and said, "Do you want to go to jail for assaulting a police officer?"

"Let go of me!" Demetrius snapped.

Frank loosened his grip, and Demetrius snatched her hand away.

She quickly gathered her composure and decided not to get into a war of insults with him. She knew she didn't have to defend herself against the assumptions of a black-hearted person like Frank. He was the very definition of the problems that started the plague of destruction in the inner city.

He would never understand the dynamics. The social structure, the love, honor, and respect that governs her neighborhood. Developed out of poverty and the injustice that the system caused. He would never understand the sense of responsibility that's embedded in the elders for the youth, kin or not. In the streets or not, they still protected and supported their own.

Inhaling a deep breath through her nostrils, she composed her thoughts and said, "I'm not intimidated by you, Frank, you don't scare me, and it wouldn't be in your best interest to underestimate me because I'm much more than what my past may suggest. So please don't let it mislead you because it will take you down a path that you won't come back from, and that's a threat. Now my Godson is in the hospital on life support, and I need to be there by his side. I have nothing further to say to you or any other detectives. Whatever information you need, you have to hit the pavement and beat ya feet!"

Demetrius stood up from the table. "Now, unless I'm under arrest, I would like to leave!" she added.

"Well, it's not for me to excuse you. That would be for the lead Detectives Washington or Williams," Frank said.

Frank stood as well, having heard enough and knowing that the interview wasn't going anywhere.

"I'ma leave you with these parting words Demetrius. You just made an enemy for yourself, your Godson, and that fraudulent nonprofit. That's a threat!" Franks said and walked toward the door.

"Well, I look forward to our next encounter, Frank. For your sake, let's hope it's not on my turf!" she responded as he walked through the door.

* * *

The other day Alfonso was brainstorming. While going through his Rolodex of telephone numbers, he came across his old pastor 'Carlos Ruiz. He wondered how Pastor Ruiz and the congregation at his church would be doing. They were like one big family, as he remembered attending bible study and the after-school programs.

He contemplated going because he knew Pastor Ruiz would invite him to attend church services, and Alfonso wasn't sure if he was ready for that kind of commitment right now, but he had to call, so he did.

The Pastor was pleased to speak to Alfonso. Happy to find out that he and Rebecca were doing good and surprised to find out that he became a police officer. Alfonso thought that Pastor Ruiz would ask why he stopped attending church, and he struggled to come up with an answer but was relieved when the Pastor didn't ask.

After a lengthy conversation and a few scriptures from the bible, the Pastor finally asked Alfonso to join services next Sunday. Alfonso agreed. He didn't want to hurt the Pastor's feelings by declining.

Before hanging up the phone, out of curiosity, Alfonso asked the pastor if he knew any Nicaraguan immigrants. The pastor was silent for a long second before asking if it had anything to do with his police work. Alfonso noticed how the delightful tone of his voice turned to worry and concern. Alfonso knew the Pastor wouldn't go on record about anything. He knew about the streets and feared retaliation, just like what happened to his grandparents. So Alfonso told him that whatever they talked about would be strictly between the two of them. With that assurance, the pastor told him that he knew of a few and agreed to talk to him if it would help.

The church was located in the Badlands, a few blocks away from where Alfonso grew up. He tried to avoid driving through this section of the city because of all the memories it would bring back of his childhood with Rebecca and his grandparents. Memories that almost drove him to commit suicide because of the pain of losing them. As he drove through the neighborhood and reflected, it didn't cause him as much grief as he thought. His heart and soul were getting stronger, which meant he was doing the right thing on the right path in his life.

He was overcome with a sense of pride because he knew that his grandparents would be proud of what he had become. He felt grateful to have been blessed with the family that he had, no matter how much time they had to spend together.

He smiled at the field his grandfather took him to kick around the soccer ball or for him and Rebecca to ride their bikes. The corner store his grandmother took him to after school to buy snacks. The swimming pool they went to in the summer, and the playgrounds with the sliding boards and swings. He could remember the images so vividly that it felt like he was watching a movie.

Alfonso drove down the block he used to live on and noticed that their old house was just a lot now, a gap in between two other houses burned beyond repair and knocked down by the City of Philadelphia. He wanted to walk on the grass where the house once stood to try and see if he could feel the essence of his grandparents, but he decided not to. He knew that their essence followed him and Rebecca everywhere they were.

When he got to the church, he found Pastor Ruiz in his office waiting for him.

"Alfonso, man, it's good to see you!" Pastor Ruiz said, shaking his hand and embracing him in a hug.

"It's good to see you too, sir!" Alfonso responded after they broke their embrace.

"Man, look at you, son! How many years has it been?" the pastor asked while taking a step back to size Alfonso up.

"Too many to count," Alfonso answered.

"God is good, isn't He, Alfonso? He never burdens us with more than we can stand, and as soon as we feel we are gonna break, he blesses us with the strength to straighten our backs and throw the weight of those burdens off our shoulders. Everything that happens is the creed of God. He tests our will and our might, and our virtue, and it's up to us to learn the lessons and to gain the wisdom that comes from our experiences! It's good to see you back, Alfonso!" Pastor Ruiz said.

They sat down and talked about the old times, reminisced on memories and events, retold funny stories, laughed, and joked. They talked about the present times and caught each other up on where they were currently in life. The condition of the church and its members.

There was a program available to the kids, and the Pastor asked Alfonso to help by volunteering and just being a positive male figure for the kids to look up to. Alfonso agreed to devote as much time and to help as much as he could. Not because he didn't want to hurt the Pastor's feelings but because he felt it was his duty and obligation to give back to the ones that gave him.

Then Alfonso got to the reason he was there.

"Maria Munoz, have you ever heard of her?" he asked.

The Pastor rubbed the hair on his chin and nodded, then said, "Ah, Maria Munoz! I don't know her personally, but I know a lot about her!"

"Could you please tell me what you know about her, Pastor? Rumors and all because it's really important!" Alfonso said.

The Pastor looked Alfonso in his eyes and asked, "Off the record?"

"Off the record. What you tell me will never leave this room, sir. You have my word!" Alfonso answered.

The pastor took a deep breath and began to speak. Alfonso listened attentively without interrupting.

"A lot of Hispanics that migrated to Philadelphia came to the badlands because this is the city's Hispanic community, and Maria Munoz was no exception. There was a handful of Maria Munoz's living in the badlands around the time she arrived, so she was nicknamed 'Nikki Munoz', short for Nicaraguan Munoz. Only a few people have met her or even know what she looked like, and the majority of them are dead now.

"At that time, a lot of people around here heard of Nikki Munoz. Her name was synonymous with cocaine and murder.

"When she got to the Badlands in 1994, she quickly found out about all the drug dealers that controlled the drug market around here. Then she hand-picked a dealer of her own. A twenty-three-year-old kid named 'Gabriel Rodriguez' a.k.a 'Gabi!'" He had no connections with any of the top suppliers, and Nikki only supplied one person at a time. In order for her to corner the market, set a precedent, and establish her laws on how the drug game was going to be run in the badlands while she was around, She had to get rid of the competition, and anybody that she felt was gonna be a threat. She put together what was called 'The Body List.' A list of 15 people that she felt stood in her way of taking and controlling the drug game.

"She brought two killers to the Badlands called 'The Hit Team.' They were also Nicaraguan immigrants and former soldiers of the Rebel National Army of Nicaragua. She funded the war campaign and supplied the guns and vehicles, safe houses, and locations of the people on the body list.

"Gabi and the hit team murdered all 15 people in what became the first drug war of the 90s in the Badlands, spawning 155 other murders that same year as a direct result and aftermath. Leaving the drug game basically decimated in the Badlands, the mayor of Philadelphia threatened to send the National Guards to police the area if the violence didn't stop.

"The following year, her dealer, 'Gabi,' rose to power. She supplied him with the best and cheapest bricks of cocaine that were available in the Tri-State area for him to rebuild the structure of the drug game under her instructions.

"Gabi's run lasted for seven years, and it was reported that he made anywhere between 300 to 400 million dollars before he became the subject of a federal indictment in 2002.

"Instead of Maria taking a chance on Gabi not cooperating with the feds, she had him and 6 of his associates murdered over four days. More than likely, all the associates were all people who knew enough to implement her in the indictment. All 7 of their decapitated heads were found in a deep freezer at Gabi's $3,500,000 mansion in Montgomery County, as well as 10 bricks of cocaine and $950,000 in cash. The bodies were never recovered.

"Then, as quickly as Maria came, saw, and conquered, she was gone!" Pastor Ruiz told him.

Alfonso couldn't believe what he was hearing about the frail, angelic-looking woman that he saw in her driver's license photo. She kinda favored his grandmother or one of the older ladies that did volunteer work at the church when he was younger. It was hard for him to imagine her being capable of doing what he was just told.

After the pastor finished speaking, he just sat there silent for a minute or two, trying to compute the information and figure out where to start first with his questions for the pastor.

"Some story, huh?" the Pastor asked after seeing Alfonso at a loss for words.

Alfonso couldn't respond because he had heard of Gabi when he was a kid and remembered what it was like growing up in the badlands during those years.

After gathering his thoughts, he said, "It's a hell of a story! Excuse my language, but did you hear anything about her having any family like a brother?"

"No family, not to my knowledge!" Pastor Ruiz answered.

"If you don't mind me asking, how do you know all this?" Alphonso asked.

The pastor smiled and said, "I wasn't always a Pastor, you know. A few friends I had before I devoted my life to the Lord kept in touch with me over the years. Sometimes one would confide in me with their problems, even repeated gossip a time or two. Plus, you know it's my community, so I kinda keep my ears to the streets to see what was going on!"

"Do you know what she's doing now or where she moved to?" Alfonso asked.

"She's probably wherever the first drug war broke out in Philadelphia after 2002," Pastor Ruiz answered.

Right, Alfonso thought and kinda felt stupid for asking that question and not figuring it out himself.

"I don't believe it's true, but I heard three years ago she had two tractor-trailers full of clothes and supplies delivered to a women's shelter on Second and Front Street," Pastor Ruiz said.

"Could I have the name of the shelter, please?" Alfonso asked.

"Cita's Women and Children Center," the pastor answered.

"You've been a great help, pastor, and I enjoyed our talk, but I have some work to get started on. I look forward to joining services on Sunday and meeting the congregation!" Alfonso said, standing.

Pastor Ruiz stood as well

"Between us, right? Because I don't want my name attached to anything that has something to do with Maria," Pastor Ruiz said.

"You have my word, sir!" Alfonso assured him.

With that, they shook hands, and Alfonso left with way more than he could've hoped for. He wondered if Frank knew this story about her, and if not, what did Frank know in order for him to GPS her car in a failed attempt to track her? He also wondered what was Frank's next move because he had his and was one up on the investigation into Maria Munoz.

Chapter 13

June Bug was Kirk's 73-year-old uncle who worked as a tractor-trailer driver most of his life. He knew the highways and the back roads like the back of his hand. From 1990 to 1994, he was paid by a mid-level drug cartel in Arizona to transport tons of weed and cocaine to Atlanta.

He had long retired from driving tractor-trailers and now owned several mobile homes that he rented to families going on vacations. He didn't make much money, rarely any at all. When he first invested in the mobile homes business, he thought it was a good idea, but now with the Pandemic wrecking the Country, it was just something to pass the time.

When Kirk first got into the drug game, June bug told him he would be there to assist him in any way he could. So when Kirk and Shane asked if they could modify some of his mobile homes with secret stash compartments to transport their drugs, June bug let them. He even offered to run the route for them since driving was his profession, and they agreed.

It wasn't about the money for June bug. He did it for the thrill of living his life again. In his old age, he wasn't living for nothing, and would die with no regrets when his time came.

Shane and Kirk called June bug, and he transported everything to the Hit Factory. The 300 bricks of cocaine and the 100 bricks of fentanyl were successfully cut and compressed at the Hit Factory.

Now they were laid up at a hotel in Miami with a fist full of to keep them, company women.

"Look at me, baby!" Shane said to Melissa, a Puerto Rican bombshell with her face buried in his lap, giving him a blow job.

She stopped to look at him, his dick still in her mouth.

Shane rubbed his hand over her head and through her silky blond hair and said, "You know you beautiful, baby, right?"

Mellisa nodded without removing his dick from her mouth.

"Now, I don't want to be looking at the top of the back of your head when you have those amazing eyes and that gorgeous face for me to look at. Don't be ashamed to look at me, baby. I'm a boss, and this a self-made multi-million dollar dick you got in ya mouth, you hear me?" Shane told her.

Mellisa nodded again, batting her long eyelashes at him, her luscious pink lips still wrapped around the head of his dick like a lollipop.

"Be proud of yourself, baby. You might never get a chance to taste something this expensive again. You don't have to rush. Go ahead and savor the moment!" Shane said to her.

"Mellisa's mouth was making a popping sound as she pulled his dick from between her lips and said, "Yes, Papi!" Then she put his dick back in her mouth and did what she was told.

"Papi, you being mean! I want to taste some of that million-dollar dick too!" Angela said, his second Puerto Rican bombshell while kissing and licking his neck and chest.

Mellisa popped Shane's dick out her mouth and said, "It's a multi-million-dollar dick, bitch!" Then went back to her business.

"That's right, baby!" Shane whispered and rubbed Mellisa's head.

"Can I have some, Papi?" Angela begged.

"You gotta wait until Mellisa's done unless she wants to share," Shane said, sinking deeper into the plush pillows that were propping him up on the California king mattress.

"That bitch stingy!" Angela whined.

"Um, umm!" Mellisa slurped and moaned, teasing Angela.

"What it tastes like bitch, since you want to be greedy!" Angela snapped.

Mellisa popped his dick out of her mouth again and said, "It tastes good, bitch, just like money!" Then she put his dick back in her mouth and started to tease Angela again.

"That's not fair, Papi!" Angela protested.

"Let me see if you are ready yet, baby!" Shane said to Angela.

She opened her legs to invite him. He put his hand in between them to feel her juicy, wet pussy, throbbing with anticipation.

"This pussy is ready for you, Papi!" Angela said, biting her bottom lip, twisting her hips, and grinding her pussy up against Shane's fingers as he massaged her clit.

"Yea, it's almost ready. You want this dick in you, baby?" Shane asked her.

"Ooh, Papi, I want that dick in me. I need that dick in my life, Papi. I need you to put all that fat dick inside my tight pussy and bust it open, Papi. I want to ride that multi-million dollar dick like a good bitch!" Angela said, still grinding her pussy against Shane's fingers, trying to steal a quick nut.

Shane pulled his hand away, her pussy juice all over his fingers, dripping down his diamond rings and his knuckles.

"Almost, baby, but not yet," Shane said.

"Ooh, Papi, why are you mean to me, Papi?" Angela pleaded.

Mellisa popped Shane's dick out of her mouth and stuck her tongue out at Angela in a mocking gesture, then slurped his dick back in her mouth to finish.

"Be patient, baby. We're here all weekend. Ya'll gon' get a rich amount of this multi-million-dollar dick!" Shane said as Angela went back to kissing and licking all over his neck and chest.

* * *

"Yo, cousin!" Kirk said into the phone while standing in the living room of the presidential suite with the curtains drawn back on the glass window, looking out at the beach.

"Yea, man, what's up with you?" Chris, the person on the other end of the phone, said back to Kirk.

"I'm just checking in with you. Make sure you are ok!" Kirk said.

"Where Shane at? I called his phone, but it went straight to his voice mail," Chris asked.

"I don't even know why he got a phone because he never answered it. You won't hear from him unless he calls you!" Kirk said.

"Yea, well, you know. I usually deal with him, like, everything cool?" Chris asked.

"Yeah, everything is smooth. He tied up right now. That's why I'm calling. If it's a problem, you could just wait around until he gets time to return your call. It's not a big deal. Just trying to make sure you don't get left out!" Kirk said to him.

Chris was one of Shane's customers. Kirk had him on a tapped phone conversation with the feds. He was setting up Chris to buy the drugs from a federal agent in hopes he would get arrested and ultimately cooperate in the indictment against Shane also.

"I guess that's cool. What's the play?" Chris asked.

Kirk had him where he wanted him. *It was too easy*, he thought.

He put his palms against the glass window and continued to stare out at the beach and the ocean. It was a beautiful day. The sky was clear and blue.

A few years ago, he could've never imagined that his life would have turned out the way it had. He was winning, this was the high point in his life, but he knew the bottom was coming. With the witness protection program the feds had set up for him, plus the money he managed to stash without Shane knowing, he knew he would be able to bounce back.

"Ima send you an address. My guy gone meet you there. Same thing as before, just shoot me a text when you are outside," Kirk told him.

"Ard bet. Ima see if my homie is trying to score, so I might have some extra money," Chris said.

"That's cool. Whatever he need it's there for him," Kirk said.

"Ok!" Chris replied, then they both hung up the phone.

* * *

“You got that?” Federal Agent Fisher asked his communications technician after listening to Kirk and Chris’s phone conversation through a wiretap.

“I got it, and I’m making a copy as we speak!”

“We still got the tail on Chris, right?” Agent Fisher asked.

“Like white on rice!” the technician answered.

“Perfect!” Agent Fisher said.

CHAPTER 14

"From the bullet wounds to his right forearm, it seems as though he put his arms up to shield himself. The bullet entered his forearm, crushing the bone on its way through, then grazed his face below his right eye, leaving a deep laceration and fracturing his cheekbone. If it wasn't for him putting his arm up and reflecting the trajectory of the bullet, it surely would've entered his face and been fatal," Doctor Prescot said to Demetrius. They were in Chance's hospital room at university.

Demetrius looked down at Chance, who was still in a medically induced coma and on a breathing machine. She could barely recognize him because of how badly his face was swollen.

"As you can see, the swelling is severe on the right side of his face and around the right eye. Usually, when the eye is that swollen, it pinches the nerves in the back of the eye. If the swelling is not relieved, it can cause damage to the eyesight. We're afraid that we won't be able to get him into surgery in time to relieve that pressure!" Doctor Prescot said.

"Why not?" Demetrius asked.

"If we go back in before the swelling goes down on its own, it might add more pressure to his brain. If that was to happen, he will need another surgery in which we would have to remove part of his skull to relieve that pressure. That could possibly cause him to slip into a coma or maybe sustain some kind of brain damage!" Doctor Prescot answered.

Demetrius's mouth dropped open. She was so overwhelmed with grief that she was at a loss for words. She just stared at the doctor, tryna hold back her tears.

Her mind flashed back to when Hammer pulled up in front of the house, beeping the car horn and banging on the front door.

"Oh my God!" she said as she opened the door and was startled by the look of horror on Hammer's face.

She looked at the car double parked in the middle of the street, riddled with bullet holes. The passenger side door was open, and she saw a body crumpled in the seat. Although she couldn't see the face, she knew it was Chance, and from all the bullet holes in the car, she knew he was shot. Her heart instantly fell to the bottom of her stomach.

"Mama! Chance got shot. You gotta get him to the hospital!" Hammer yelled at her hysterically.

It took her brain a fraction of a second to assess the situation and the reason Hammer brought him to her instead of taking him to the hospital himself.

“Grab my car keys!” she yelled back as she ran out of the house to the car, wearing only a bathrobe, socks, and a scarf wrapped around her hair.

When she leaned in and saw Chance’s bloody, motionless body, she feared that it was too late, and he was already dead. It took everything in her not to scream out in agony.

Hammer ran back over with her car keys.

“Help me get him in the back seat!” she demanded.

Hammer reached into the car and picked up Chance, cradling him in his arms and against his chest like a baby.

Demetrius watched the blood spill from Chance’s body as Hammer carried him to her car and put him in the back seat.

“Get rid of that car, Hammer. Leave it in the garage around the corner. Then go into the house and stay there. Don’t answer the door or the phone for nobody!” she said as she climbed into the driver’s seat of her car, started the engine, and pulled off.

She prayed that it wasn’t too late, and that Chance was still alive by the time she reached the hospital.

* * *

“Ms. Douglas!” Doctor Prescot said. Bringing her back to the present moment.

“I know this is a lot for you to take right now, and I could only imagine how you might feel. I could come back another time to inform you of your godson's condition if that will help," Doctor Prescot finished.

Demetrius gathered herself and pulled some strength from deep within and said, "No, no, I'm fine, Dr. Prescot. I need to know what happened to my baby so I can start preparing to get him better. Please continue!"

She knew the worst was over no matter how devastating Chance's injuries were. He was gonna live, and that was the only thing that mattered. Any other problems would have to be dealt with as they occurred, one step at a time.

"Another bullet entered his shoulder where his rotator cup is and exited through his back, an inch above his shoulder blade. The bullet tore the nerves that give feeling and movement to his right hand. We tried to repair as much of the damaged nerves as we could, but he may have limited mobility with the use of it. We won't know the extent until everything starts to heal. You know everybody heals differently. He'll need another surgery and extensive rehabilitation therapy also!" Doctor Prescot said.

The doctor paused to see how well Demetrius was taking the information on Chance's injury before he continued.

She nodded, letting him know she was fine and urging him to finish.

"Another bullet entered the right side of his chest by the collar bone and exited through his back. No nerves, arteries, or organs were damaged. The final bullet went through his right side, breaking two ribs, puncturing and collapsing his right lung before embedding itself 3 centimeters away from his spinal cord. That was the difficult surgery because if the bullet moved even a fraction of an inch, it would have paralyzed him, but we were successful in removing it!" Doctor Prescot said.

"Thank God!" Demetrius said.

"Because of all the blood loss, we had to give him a transfusion. His condition seems to be stabilizing, and his heartbeat is getting stronger. From the scan of his brain, it's looking pretty active. I'm assuming that within the next couple of days, he should be coming out of the coma and off the life support machine if he keeps improving. He won't be able to speak verbally because of his face injury and will have to be on a liquid diet," Doctor Prescot told her.

"But he is going to pull through, right?" Demetrius asked.

"That's what we're hoping for. His chances look good. He's a strong young man, Ms. Demetrius!" Doctor Prescot said.

"Thank you, Doctor," she said, reaching out to shake his hand.

"Don't worry about it. Just doing my job. You have my card. If you have any concerns or questions, feel free to call!" he told her.

"I will if I need to, and thanks again for everything!" she said. Then the doctor turned and left the hospital room.

"I'm here, baby. I'm not going anywhere, Chance! You hear me. We are leaving this hospital together!" Demetrius said to Chance, holding his left hand and closing her eyes as tears began to fall from her face.

* * *

Hammer was locked inside Mama Meechie's bathroom, pacing back and forth and chain-smoking cigarettes. He was going through an episode and talking to the two voices he heard inside his head and imagined were real people.

"Look at him. He's bitching!" Shaun said. He was the first voice and imaginary person Hammer saw. He was standing in the corner of the bathroom smoking a cigarette.

"He's not bitching. He's just tryna figure out his next move," Phil said, the second voice in Hammer's head that he imagined was a person. He was leaning against the bathroom sink.

"You better watch your mouth! I told you, I don't do any bitching!" Hammer yelled at Shaun, stopping his pacing to point a finger at him, then going back to pacing.

"My fault, playa!" Shaun said, holding his hands in the air. "I'm just wondering what you tryna figure out because we already know what the next move is!"

"Yeah, but don't you think we should fall back while Chance is in the hospital?" Phil asked.

"Fall back for what? We ain't never need Chance to make a move!" Shaun snapped.

"What if something goes wrong? Who gon' hold Chance down?" Phil asked.

"If something goes wrong? What the fuck is gon' go wrong? Cause the only thing I see wrong is this nigga bitching!" Shaun yelled while pointing at Hammer.

"What the fuck, I tell you?" Hammer yelled back at Shaun while walking up to him.

Hammer hated to be called a bitch or to be called scared.

He grabbed Shaun by the front of his shirt and raised his fist to punch him.

"Chill, Hammer!" Phil said.

Hammer dropped his fist and said, "I'll break your jaw next time you disrespect me!"

He let Shaun's shirt go, then started back pacing.

"Damn, playa! After the last time, you promised not to hit me again!" Shaun said.

"Promises are meant to be broken!" Phil said.

"Jaws are too!" Hammer said, glancing at Shawn out of the corner of his eye.

"I'm just saying. We can't let that shit ride another day. Somebody gotta pay for that shit tonight!" Shaun said.

"What we tryna figure out is who gon' pay!" Phil counters.

"I don't give a fuck who it is! We gotta send somebody home. We gotta go out there and start killing niggas to make a statement, some shit like that. Somebody gon' die every day until somebody lets us know who shot Chance or had something to do with it!" Shaun yelled, pounding a fist into his palm.

"Shhh, somebody gon' hear you, you talking too loud!" Hammer said, lighting another cigarette.

"I forgot. It's my fault," Shaun apologized.

"You're on the right path Shaun, but it's something we are missing!" Phil said.

"I know who we can start with!" Shaun said.

"Who?" Phil asked.

"Them bitch ass Youngbulls holding the block down for us. They find out Chance got shot and just disappear with the money and the work. They basically robbed us. What type of shit is that? We should kill them mufuckas!" Shaun yelled.

"Shhh, you hear that?" Hammer said, putting his ear to the door to listen.

Shaun and Phil came over to do the same.

"I don't hear anything!" Phil said.

"Somebody coming, it sounds like!" Hammer said.

"Ain't nobody home Hammer, Mama Meechie at the hospital with Chance!" Phil assured him.

"See, this is what I'm talking about! Somebody almost shot your little brother to death, and you are here acting like a nut!" Shaun yelled at him.

Hammer went into a blind rage. He grabbed Shaun by the neck and slammed him all over the bathroom, knocking all the toiletries and hygiene products off the shelves and breaking the vanity mirror before getting Shaun in the corner and kicking him.

"Ahhh, Ahhh! Robert, stop hitting me!" Shaun screamed.

As Shaun called Hammer his stepfather's name, Robert, Shaun turned into a seven-year-old image of Hammer lying in the corner getting beat by his stepfather Robert.

Hammer stopped and just stared at the seven-year-old image of himself in the corner, bloody and crying.

Phil placed a hand on Hammer's shoulder and changed his voice to Hammer's mother, and yelled, "Stop, Robert! That's enough, please!"

Hammer jumped back at the icy touch of Phil's hand on his shoulder and his mother's voice in his ear calling him his stepfather's name.

"I'm not Robert. I'm not Robert!" Hammer screamed, backing away from the beaten and bloody image of his 7-year-old self.

He looked in the broken vanity mirror and saw his stepfather's face looking back at him instead of his own.

"Stop! Stop!" he screamed and then punched the broken mirror, shattering it more and cutting his hand.

He backed away and stumbled into the bathtub, falling into it and pulling the shower curtain down with him. He got up and stumbled into a corner of the bathroom away from Phil and Shaun.

Shaun got off the floor, and he was his regular self again. He and Phil walked toward Hammer, both talking in high-pitched voices at the same time.

Hammer couldn't understand anything they were saying, and the pitch of their voice made his head and his ears hurt.

"Shut the fuck up!" he screamed, putting his hands over his ears. "Shut the fuck up!"

He closed his eyes and slumped to the floor in the corner.

A second later, everything went silent. When he opened his eyes, he saw a memory of his past in 3rd person.

"Brother, brother, wake up!" A 5-year-old Chance said to his 7-year-old brother while standing next to his bed and shaking his shoulder.

Hammer's eyes watered, and tears began to fall from his face as he saw his little brother standing there. He reached out to grab him and hug him but came up with nothing. It was just a memory of his past he was relieving.

"Brother! James, wake up, please. Mom and Robert were fighting again. Wake up!" Chance said.

James was woken and heard them fighting like he did every night but chose to lay there and ignore it, pretending like he was asleep. There was nothing he could do. Every time he tried to stop his stepfather from beating on his mom, he got beat instead, and his mom did little to stop it.

Tonight, was different. He couldn't ignore it. His little brother heard it and wanted him to do something about it.

Chance looked up to him. They depended on each other. They had no other friends, so they were each other's best friend. How could he tell him to go back to bed and block Mommy's crying out because there was nothing they could do. How could he tell him he was scared to go see what was going on because he didn't want to get beaten by his stepfather again? How could he tell him that they couldn't protect Mommy? He couldn't. If his little brother wanted to see, he could see. If their stepfather got mad, then he would just have to take another beating. This time for his little brother's curiosity. So he rolled over and pretended to just have woken up.

"What's wrong?" he asked.

"Mom and Robert were just fighting. I think she's in the bathroom crying. We gotta go help her brother. Come on!" Chance said, pulling on his arm.

James climbed out of bed and followed Chance out of the bedroom and into the hallway. They tiptoed to the bathroom door and placed their ears against it to listen.

"Can you hear her?" Chance whispered as they listened to her sobbing and talking to herself.

"Yea, I hear her!" James whispered back.

"Who's in there with her? Who is she talking to?" Chance asked.

"I don't know!" James answered.

This was not the first time he listened at the bathroom door to his mom cry and talk to herself as if somebody was in there with her.

"Let's look in!" Chance whispered.

James slowly turned the knob and cracked the door open a little so they could peek in. Their mom was standing at the sink in front of the mirror, crying. Her clothes were torn, her hair was in disarray, and she had a wet rag wiping her beaten, bloody and swollen face. In between sobs, she would talk to herself in the mirror as if she was holding a conversation with another person. Then she would break down and cry again.

James and Chance froze at the sight of her. They were too young to comprehend how she could allow herself to be used and abused that way.

As Hammer watched the memory of his mother, he reached out to touch her, to hold her, to hug her, calling out her name, "Mom, Mom," but came out with nothing again.

The tears started to fall from his eyes uncontrollably.

"Close that damn door and go to bed!" Their mother screamed at them, turning and noticing them peeking in through the door.

James closed the door, and they stood there for a few seconds in silence.

"You see what he did to her!" Chance whispered through clenched teeth, tears rolling down his face. Fuming with anger that a 5-year-old shouldn't have to feel.

"I wish I was big enough to fuck him up!" James told him.

"Come on. I know how we can get him!"Chance said.

James followed Chance through the hallway and back into their bedroom. Chance climbed under James's bed and came back out with an old rusty construction hammer that they played with in the backyard. They used it to break everything they could find.

Chance gave it to James and said, "Fuck him up with this!"

James took the hammer from Chance and looked at it. He knew how easily it broke glass bottles or the TV they beat to rubble. How he saw some kids use the claw side to tear out the bottom of milk crates to make basketball hoops. He knew what this hammer could do to his stepfather.

"Come on!" Chance said.

James followed him out of the room and back into the hallway. They tiptoed into their mom's bedroom, where their stepfather was in bed, sound asleep and snoring. An empty liquor bottle sat next to the bed on the floor.

James stood there frozen for a few seconds. He was scared.

"Go hit him," Chance whispered.

James didn't move.

"Give it to me. I'll do it!" Chance whispered, trying to take the hammer, but James wouldn't let it go.

Then a voice came into James's head and said, "If you don't do it, he just gon' keep beating on you and your mom, and you know who gon' be next. Don't be scared of that mufucka. He ain't nobody. Fuck him up like he fuck you up!"

That little voice, even though he didn't know where it came from, gave him enough courage to do it. Eventually, that voice turned into two. Shaun was the first, and Phil was the second.

He walked over to the bed, then looked back at Chance and saw him smiling. His head leaned forward, and his chinky eyes focused on watching the hammer's destruction of Robert's face.

James looked down at his stepfather, raised the hammer, and aimed it at his forehead. As he began to bring the hammer down with as much force as he could, his stepfather opened his eyes.

Hammer jumped out of the memory, dizzy and disoriented as he tried to get a grasp of where he was at. Once he gathered himself, he realized he was still in Mama Meechie's bathroom, sitting in the corner. His eyes and cheeks were wet from crying, and he felt a throbbing sensation in his hand.

He looked at it and, for the first time, noticed the deep gash on his knuckle. He looked around the bathroom and saw that it was trashed. Hammer knew he did it but couldn't remember how and why. He just knew that Mama Meechie was gonna be pissed.

Hammer knew he had an episode and knew he was out of it and that it was the first time it had happened without Chance, but he couldn't remember anything, not even how he got in the bathroom.

He got up off the floor, wiped the tears off his face, and grabbed a towel to wrap his hand up. He couldn't sit around and wait like Mama Meechie wanted him to. He had to hit the streets and find out who had tried to kill him and his little brother. He was going to kill them and everything close to them. The first person he was going to start with was the last person they talked to, John.

CHAPTER 15

"Frank! It took you long enough, fat fuck!" David Cameron said. He was Frank's former partner on the police force, now commissioner and head of Frank's extortion business. They were meeting in a parking garage at the King of Prussia mall.

"I had to kick my little sidekick first, and then the traffic was stiffer than my last old lady in the sack!" Frank said, walking up to David and shaking his hand.

"Why did you marry her then?" David asked.

"Cause her blow job was wet and sloppy, and she could bake a good potato and make a good steak!" Frank said, and they both laughed.

Frank handed David a bag and said, "It's 30 grand in there, your half of the 60 so far!"

David grabbed the bag and threw it in the back seat of his car without looking in it and asked, "So what's going on with this Alfonso kid?"

"Worse than trying to shit a hot and spicy burrito with a bad case of hemorrhoids, but he's not as clingy as he was in the beginning. You know he's getting used to the way things are, so he's a little comfortable moving around on his own now. That still doesn't change the funny feeling I have about him. He just seems too sneaky, and I don't like the way he watches me out of the corner of his eye!" Frank answered.

"Well, keep a close eye on him to see what he's up to. It does seem kind of odd for him to be so adamant about being involved in your business, then for him to just back off the way he did. Has he still been asking a ton of questions?" David asked.

"No," Frank answered.

"Not even about the GPS," David asked.

"Never mentioned it once," Frank answered.

"Doesn't that seem strange? You think he's Internal Affairs?" David asked, a little concerned.

"Anything is possible, but I doubt it. He doesn't seem to be that smart!" Frank said, trying to assure him.

"Well, something else definitely got his attention, and I think you should find out what it is, can't trust new cops as far as you can throw 'em. They all seemed to believe in the system and are willing to sacrifice their own lives to prove it!" David said.

"Tell me something I don't know?" Frank said.

"Kirk borough and Shane white!" David answered.

"Who the fuck are them, and why should I know them?" Frank asked.

"Let's sit in the car!" David said, then hopped in the driver's seat of his Chevy Impala.

Frank hopped in the passenger seat.

"My sources told me that Maria Munoz is supplying Shane and Kirk and had been doing so for the last 7 years," David said.

"Your sources? You never told me you had a source!" Frank said with an attitude.

"Yeah, well, it was a need-to-know basis, and at that time, you didn't need to know!" David told him.

"You can save all the hip talk! We don't keep secrets and hide sources of information from each other!" Frank said.

"I wasn't keeping a secret or hiding anything. At that time, I wasn't sure if the information being provided was gonna be real and of value or just some more of that bullshit we've been getting!" David said.

"So that's how you found out about the green Suburban?" Frank asked.

"Yea!" David answered.

"Well, who the hell is it, and what's the deal?" Frank asked.

David took a deep breath and said, "Her name is Kenya Bradshaw. She's one of Kirk Borough's girlfriends!"

"One of them?" Frank asked.

"Yea, you know. A guy like him with a lot of money got a lot of women!" David said.

"How long was she one of them?" Frank asked.

"She was the first. They've been together since high school before he started dealing!" David answered.

"Scorned, huh! Mad about all the new women!" Frank said.

"Exactly! He pushes her off to the side and tells her she'll be lucky if she sees or talks to him once a week now. He had her living a certain lifestyle that she's struggling to maintain without him!" David said.

"No kids?" Frank asked.

"A miscarriage and two abortions," David answered.

"So there's nothing to keep him connected to her except secrets. If he could stop seeing her altogether if he wanted," Frank said.

"That's why she's afraid of losing her main source of income. Plus, she feels betrayed since she's been there since the beginning. Check this out. Kirk's a pillow talker. Brags about the people he knows and the moves he makes. That's how he builds his confidence with the ladies in the bedroom. From what she said, he can't keep it up in bed, so he impresses them with talk!" David said, then wiped a bead of sweat off his eyebrow.

"Limp dick, huh?" Frank said with a chuckle.

"Whatever you want to call it, buddy. Anyway, she figures since she knows some information, she might as well cash in on it while she can!" David added.

"Unbelievable!" Frank said, taking a moment to think about if he told any of his ex-wives information that he shouldn't. He couldn't recall but knew he would never and dismissed the thought. Then he wondered if maybe David did a little pillow talking to impress the ladies. Frank hoped he didn't and decided he was going to ask him to be sure when the time was right.

"So, how did you meet her?" Frank asked.

"Come to find out, Kirk knows about us!" David answered.

"Really? Well, why didn't we know about him?" Frank asked.

"You know Mack, the dealer from 53rd and Greenway, who's on our books for $1,500 a week?" David asked.

"Yea!" Frank answered.

"You know Steve from 30th and Susquehanna? He's in our books, the guy from Lansdowne Ave, Lancaster Ave, Germantown Ave!" David said.

"Get to the fucking point, Dave!" Frank shouts.

"Basically, 80% of all the guys we are taxing. Their suppliers are being supplied by Kirk and Shane. They definitely heard about us, and the reason we haven't heard about them is because we're operating our business 3 levels below them!" David said.

"So all this time, we think we are doing something, and the little money we get is just pocket change!" Frank said.

"Basically, since they control 80% of the cocaine market in Philadelphia, and we haven't even checked the rest of the Tri-State area!" David said.

The news made Frank feel like a succa because he and David were slipping. A decade ago, they had their hands in the pockets of all the big dogs in the city, from the cocaine dealers to the heroin, the barbiturates, and down to the weed. If there were somebody making enough money, Frank took some from them, and if he couldn't get his slice of the pie, he helped put them behind bars rather with the state or the feds.

"Since Maria Munoz has been supplying Kirk and Shane, they've been the big dogs for the last 7 years. For Frank and David to just be finding out about it means they let a lottery ticket slip through their hands. All they've been getting is the scraps from the mangy mutts on the corner. This was a reality check for Frank to tighten up and get back in the game," David said.

"So I'm guessing since she heard about us, she reached out and got in contact with you?" Frank asked, now finally realizing the magnitude of the investigation and suspicious because David was holding out.

"Right!" David answered.

"And I'm assuming that you didn't even tell me half the reason I was to track the Suburban besides it being registered to Maria Munoz?" Frank asked with an attitude.

"It's not like that, Frank!" David said defensively.

"God damn it, David, as long as we've been working together, you're gonna treat me like that, like a flunky, and spoon-feed me!" Frank snapped, banging his hand on the dashboard.

"I wasn't sure if what the bitch was feeding me legit or not, Frank. You know how it is!" David said.

"Yea, I know how it is, alright!" Frank said sarcastically.

"Come on, Frank, don't get like that," David pleaded.

"What's the story with the Suburban David, and I swear to God, if you hold out on me, our friendship is over!" Frank snapped.

David took another deep breath. The conversation wasn't going as well as he had planned, but he couldn't hold out on frank any longer.

"Kenya told me that whenever Kirk made a deal, they were given certain instructions on how to package the money and was to stash it in secret compartments in a selected car out of a fleet that was provided by Maria. Kirk told her about the drop they were making in the green Suburban," David answered.

"How much was in the Suburban, David?" Frank asked through clenched teeth.

"Supposedly, $11 million!" David slowly answered.

"11 million dollars! If there was supposed to be that much money in the car, why didn't we just take the Goddamn car, David?" Frank yells, his face beat red, blood pressure rising.

"Jeez, Frank, somebody's gonna hear you!" David said, looking around. "You think if I would've believed that much money was in the car, we wouldn't have just stolen it? I didn't believe the bitch, Frank. I thought she was just caught up in the hype and overexaggerating. I thought it was at least worth planting the GPS and seeing where that took us, maybe a stash house or something. Then when the situation happened, you know, them finding it and planting it on your daughter's car, that's when I realized it was true. Kenya's pissed, said we fucked up her payday, and now wants $25,000 upfront for any more info!" David said.

Frank sat in silence, trying to comprehend what he was hearing.

"That's why I didn't tell you. I was embarrassed and ashamed that I blew it!" David added.

Frank wasn't stupid. The real reason David didn't tell him about the money and everything was that he planned on crossing him and taking it all for himself. To leave Frank to deal with Maria and her goons when they came looking for the money, but when things didn't work out the way he planned, he had to come clean. After all the years of working with David, it broke Frank's greasy heart that he would treat him that way. He would have never rated David out. Frank knew he couldn't trust David anymore, and this would forever change the dynamics of their relationship.

"So that's what the $30,000 is for?" Frank asked him.

"Yeah, $25,000 for her!" David answered.

Franks shook his head disgustedly. "We got a former bitch. That's a distant side bitch now in our pockets for $25,000!"

“Said she got an address for us, Frank. She doesn’t know if it’s money or drugs in there, but she’s sure it’s one or the other!” David said.

“And you believe her?” Frank asked.

“I have no reason not to, Frank. If we probably missed out on 11 million in a car, I’m not gonna miss out on what could possibly be in the stash house!” David said.

“So when will you get the address?” Frank asked.

“When I set up a time and place to pay her,” David answered.

“And what if it’s bullshit?” Frank asked.

“Then we fell into another huge pile of it!” David answered.

* * *

“Got ya, Frank!” Alfonso said to himself after watching Frank get out of David Cameron’s car and into his own. Then both of them left.

Alfonso was hidden across the street from the parking garage and caught the whole meeting on his camcorder.

He trailed Frank all morning after he watched him receive a call and then creep out of the office. If he wanted to find out what Frank knew or what he was up to, he had to treat him like a suspect. Find out his close associates, get his schedule and routine together and then wait until he finds a change in it.

His instinct told him to follow him this morning because he had never crept out this early, and to his surprise, it paid off. He watched Frank meet with a few drug dealers throughout the city and collect either a brown paper bag or an envelope from each one. Alfonso knew it was either money or drugs.

Frank seemed to go about his business as if he was doing nothing wrong and had nothing to hide. A far contrast to how secretive he was moving to Alfonso and a contradiction to his character. He wondered why Internal Affairs couldn't get enough evidence on Frank because he wasn't on point as he was portrayed to be. He was really sloppy unless he just got comfortable because he was off the radar for the last couple of years. Whatever the case, he had to have some kind of inside connection to have survived this long.

Just the video from the meetings with the drug dealers was enough evidence for Alfonso to turn over to Internal Affairs and start a new investigation into Frank, and the video of the meeting with David Cameron was enough to pull him into it as well.

He wanted to look into David and find out all he could about him and his relationship with Frank because he appears to be connected with the extortion business.

Alfonso decided not to turn over the videos just yet. It would be a circumstantial case at best and expose Alfonso before he could catch his great white, Maria Munoz. Instead, he was going to continue to gather as much info and collect as much evidence as he could until he was 100% sure he could score an indictment on Frank and all his co-conspirators. If the Maria Munoz case wouldn't launch his career, this one would, and if he scored on both cases, he was guaranteed success.

After taking the memory card out of the camcorder, he placed it inside a lil' plastic case to protect it and put it in his inside jacket pocket for safekeeping. The first thing he was going to do with the videos was make a copy and store it in the hard drive of his computer or either put it in a safety deposit box. He put the camcorder in the glove box, started his car, and drove off.

It was hard for him to juggle two big cases like the ones he had. It would usually take a team of investigators for each one. What made it even harder was that he couldn't confide in anybody, but the one thing it did was consume all his free time.

The time that he would usually use to sit around the house board, dwelling on the past and constantly thinking about a drink. Not a lot, just a sip to feel the burn and to warm his belly, cutting through the tension in his life. He knew, just like everybody else knew, that one sip led to two, then three, and then bottle after bottle. Being a recovering alcoholic and coming back from a deep depression that drove him to the brink of suicide, it was a constant struggle for him to maintain his sobriety and a sound state of mind.

Another thing the cases did was challenge his intellect and ambition. Tracking down leads, tracking down people, finding information and trying to tie it all together in sequence to tell a story, and trying to predict the ending and change it before the suspect or suspects could see it come to fruition.

After the meeting with Pastor Ruiz, Alfonso checked into the two leads he had on Maria Munoz. The first was finding out about the first drug war in the city of Philadelphia after 2002 because that would give him an area of the city she was most likely working in and a potential lead on who she was supplying by finding out who gained control of that area after the war.

Two weeks after thoroughly searching the police database for drug-related crimes, homicides, and arrests, then finding a section of the city they were concentrated in, then going through report after report of closed cases and open cases. Searching the daily news archives for articles related to them, then cross-referencing them and the individuals involved. Alfonso successfully pieced together a few names and chains of events that mirrored what Pastor Ruiz told him about Maria and how she takes control of the drug market.

Alfonso found out through his research that a well-known drug dealer by the name of 'Rasheed Akron' and his team of drug dealers known in the streets as the 'Dealer Boys' controlled most of the drug market uncontested in the West and the Southwest section of Philadelphia. In early 2004, a drug war occurred between Rasheed and an unknown faction. At that same time, he was the subject of a federal indictment.

In February of that year, an attempt was made on Rasheed's life. While he was coming out of his grandmother's house on the 600 block of Spruce street, two masked gunmen opened fire on him. He was struck several times in the chest but was wearing a bulletproof kevlar vest. When the shooters saw him fall, they assumed he was dead because he wasn't moving, so they ran off. It was a botched assassination.

Rasheed was playing possum, and once he heard the shooter's flea, he crawled back to his grandmother's house. Five minutes later, four cars pulled up full of his armed men and escorted him and his grandma out of the house and into one of the cars, then they left. That was the start of the war.

No reports of the incident were made to the police, and it was only brought to their attention when confidential information was told to the sergeant of the Narcotics Task Force. The sergeant sent out a few detectives to comb the streets for info related to it, and they quickly found out it was true. Nobody knew who put the hit out on Rasheed or why, and nobody had heard or seen him since the shooting.

Within the next ten days that followed, six of Rasheed's closest friends were murdered. There was a lot of speculation about who was behind it because Rasheed was well-liked and had no major problems. He wasn't a tyrant and didn't make his way to the top by spilling blood. He was a hustla and was respected by hustlas.

Rumors started to circulate that a cartel was somehow connected to it and working with a rival dealer of his tryna take control of his territory, but the rumor was never verified.

In response, Rasheed gathered a small army of shooters and declared war against everybody who ever tried to challenge him throughout his years in the drug game. All his open enemies and everybody he had suspected of harboring ill will against him, and whom he thought had a motive or the most to gain by him being pushed out the way. Since he couldn't find the wolves hiding amongst the sheep, he figured he'd just kill the whole flock.

For the next five months, all hell broke loose in West and Southwest Philadelphia. 180 people were murdered, and well over 200 were wounded by being either shot, stabbed, or beaten.

In those five months, Rasheed became a ghost, a folklore of some sort. Every Time Somebody was shot or killed, he was to blame.

It all came to an end in July of that year when Rasheed was found shot to death in the trunk of a Mercedes Benz. His body was discovered on the corner of the block that he first started hustling on, and he began to make a name for himself. Two people were passing by and noticed blood dripping from the trunk. It was said that a $250,000 tag was put on his head, and somebody close to him set him up and cashed in.

Alfonso was sure that Maria Munoz was behind all that happened, and that summer, the drug game in Philadelphia changed hands with somebody that she appointed boss. Now all Alfonso had to do was to find out whom she had appointed, and he had a good idea of where to start looking.

To be continued...

Made in the USA
Middletown, DE
23 July 2024